The Realm Between Heaven and Hell

a novel by
J.S. Turner

Library of Congress Cataloging-in-Publication Data

Turner, Jessica.
    The Realm Between Heaven and Hell/Jessica Turner
      p.   cm.
    ISBN 978-0-9829676-1-4
    1. Fiction - Mystery, Thriller & Suspense
    2. Fiction - Religion & Spirituality
    3. Literature & Fiction - Drama

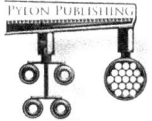

www.pylonpublishing.com

Pylon Publishing books are available at quantity discounts with bulk purchase for educational, business, or sales promotional use.

To Ms. Bertot -
Thank you for all you have taught me. You will never be forgotten.
I love you.

Special thanks to my mother for always believing in me and loving
me unconditionally, as only a mother can.
I love you.

Chapter 1

Death

Shots are fired into the darkness of the forest canopy. Hot molten lead misses her by mere inches, tearing into the surrounding trees. Shattering the bark, the shots send slivers of wood flying dangerously about her. Hounds are howling; a hunt is underway and the victim knows she is the prey.

She runs in panic through the trees, not knowing where her feet are carrying her. She can hear the snarling hounds, the cold-metal clinking of their chains that keep them tethered to their master. Her hunters' boots rustle through the dry leaves and snap the twigs and undergrowth like brittle bones. The sound of her pursuers advancing is deafening. Terror has set itself deep into every bone and crevice in her body; she knows she cannot run forever. Holding a bundle firmly to her chest, she hurdles a fallen tree, careful not to let stray branches reach the precious life wrapped within the blanket. Her arms and face are bleeding where rogue twigs and splinters have cut like glass on her smooth skin. Suddenly, the forest yields to a large field. She pauses, not wanting to leave the protection provided by the forest, not sure if she can make it to the other side. A hound's snarl snaps her neck around; her eyes grow wide. For the first time, she can see the hounds behind her. With a deep breath and a quick prayer, she bolts across the opening, her sight set on the forest on the other side. She sprints through the tall grass with ease, gaining speed and optimism with each stride. Her optimism quickly fades once she realizes the sounds of breaking twigs and crunching leaves behind her have been replaced with heavy thudding.

Her feet are light on the soft ground, and for a fleeting second, she feels free. Halfway across the field, the soft ground turns into a marshy swamp. Her feet are no longer light; they stick in the mud. It is almost as though the swamp itself were sucking her in. She lets out a wail of disbelief, desperately pulling at her legs with her free hand. She begins to sob as she realizes he is right behind her.

Two shots are fired.

The ground beneath her becomes firm again, and she continues running into the forest. She no longer hears them behind her. Somewhere in the distance she hears the howling of hounds, but she never looks back.

She eventually stops running and looks around to find herself deep within a forest. She looks up into the large oak trees and realizes she does not know where she is or how she got here, nor can she remember how long she had been running. She feels the bundle in her arms squirm and pulls the blanket down, instinctively tucking it underneath the baby's chin with her pinky finger and stroking his fat cheek with her index finger. She smiles as she looks down into his big baby-blue eyes, feeling nothing but warmth and serenity.

For some time she walks through the wilderness, admiring the tall trees and the intense, rich aroma of the forest. She looks down at the baby in her arms and smiles, as if she were in a trance. The baby squirms, uneasy, and grabs a lock of her long black hair with his chubby hand.

She looks up into the canopy at the rays of light forcing their way through the oak leaves. She knows it is still day, but the light seems to be fading. From underneath the trees, it is clear to her that night is approaching.

"I wonder what time it is," she whispers. With that thought, spoken into the stillness of the forest, comes a long, deep howling that sends chills shooting through her body. She covers the infant's face and instinctively clutches him to her chest. Frantically, she begins looking around. *I need shelter*, she thinks.

She looks through the trees, wondering which direction she should run. Another howl pierces the air. This one is definitely closer. She takes off running in the opposite direction. She has only to sprint a couple of yards before she spots a cabin. *Has that been there all along?* she wonders. The cabin is simple, and its wood is aged and beaten. *Anyone searching for me will check here*, she thinks. She then sees a flame burning in the window and hears another howl. Without another thought, she dashes for the cabin.

The young woman begins knocking on the small wooden door, softly at first, but as she hears the hounds coming ever closer, she begins knocking louder. The bundle in her firm grip begins to whine. An overwhelming fear pours over her; the howling is too close. She grabs the door handle, swings the door open and, slams the door shut behind her.

She makes herself flat against the door so as to not intrude any further into a stranger's home. She feels the old wood threatening to splinter into her back, like long, grey, unsterilized needles. The hounds are right outside the cabin now. The door jolts, forcing her forward as the hounds try to paw it down. Their howling is excruciating.

"Damn hounds." A slender woman with long black hair, braided and draped over her shoulder, comes from the back of the cabin. "Always making noise. Bark, bark, BARK!" The woman puts a candle on a wooden table in the middle of the room and begins barking at the door. She goes straight to the door, as though she doesn't even see the young woman and her baby. She places her hands on the grey, worn planks that make up the door and begins barking so ruthlessly that spit flies from the corners of her mouth. In an instant, she diverts her eyes to the woman holding the baby and politely says, "Can you please step aside, dear?" The woman does what is asked of her, taking two cautious steps to the side. Instantly, the slender woman's kind face turns back toward the hounds. She looks almost animalistic as she continues barking, her back heaving as she snarls. Reaching into her apron pocket with deliberate slowness, she pulls out a fist of what seems to be flour, letting out one last snarl before her face transforms back to reveal the tranquil woman she embodies. She blows the flour at the door, and to her satisfaction, the hounds on the other side squeal and yelp in pain. Throwing her braid back over her shoulder, she chuckles and rubs the rest of the powder off of her hands.

  "That should keep them off your back for now. Is the baby all right?"

Chapter 2

Sliver

"*H*ow did you . . . ? What . . . ? Where . . . ?" The woman struggled to ask the questions that ran through her mind. She stood still with her back to the wall, clutching the baby to her chest. She was afraid to move, frightfully aware that she knew nothing.

The woman, with the thick black braid, was now behind an island, sifting through powders, making some sort of mixture. All traces of her crazed behavior were gone. Had the barking and powder been imagined? There was a small woodstove in the corner of the kitchen, along with an old sink with no faucet and wooden cupboards that looked used and worn. In the middle of the room was a small, square, wooden table and four aged wooden chairs, each tucked properly in its place. On top of its worn surface stood a solitary candle that seemed to light the entire room.

"What is the last thing you remember, dear?" After a moment of silence, she wiped her hands on her apron and looked up from her powders. She looked at the pale-faced woman, seemingly frail and most certainly afraid; before her stood an innocent creature. Her thin arms clutched the bundle to her chest. Her scared, round, dark-blue eyes, framed most perfectly by her thick black eyebrows, darted back and forth as she tried to assess the situation. Worry lines dug deep into her wide forehead, and her full lips frowned as her chin began to quiver. She was innocent and weak.

"Dear?" the woman from behind the counter asked the fragile woman again.

"Me?" she questioned, her back still against the wall.

"There aren't any other beings in the room, dear." The woman behind the counter began sifting powders again, seeming somewhat agitated. Her movements were exact and quick. Her thick, long braid swayed as she reached left and right. She looked up through the loose black hairs that framed her face as she scooped white powder into a sack and stared at the woman by the door. Her gaze demanded an answer.

The confused woman sighed and tilted her head to the side as she tried to remember. "I . . ." Another sigh. "I remember," she paused again and stared blankly at the woman behind the counter. "I don't remember."

The woman leaned over the counter, keeping the palms of her hands on the table's corners. She leaned as far as her body would allow, never breaking the gaze she had with the other woman's bewildered eyes.

"You *need* to remember, dear," she said softly but with much command. "Try and *remember*." She seemed to be singing now. "What is the last thing you *remember*?" The word "remember" rolled hypnotically off her tongue. Her almond eyes were deep, black, and penetrating.

Nervously rocking the bundle in her arms, the seemingly younger woman became more afraid than worried. Her eyes locked on to the dark eyes of the stranger behind the counter, like a deer in headlights. She waited for the woman to speak again, to supply her with an answer. Her fear was quickly overcome by the frustration of not being able to remember anything. She broke her gaze, walked over to the wooden table that held the candle, pulled out a chair from underneath it, and wearily sat down.

Shifting the bundle from one arm to the other, she whispered to herself, "I, I don't remember anything." She pulled the blanket from the baby's face and stroked his flushed cheeks. *My little angel*, she thought. *My little Joey*. She looked up at the woman who was watching her from her post behind the counter. "Joey. His name is

Josiah."

The woman watched from behind the counter as the younger struggled to hold on to memories that were quickly slipping away. "Go on, keep going," she urged as she slowly walked to the far side of the cabin and kicked the wall three times where the cupboards met the corner. As she walked back to the table, she realized the younger woman hadn't even noticed. She sat with her body hunched over the baby, staring deeply into the orange flame of the candle. "What's your *name*, dear," she repeated sweetly from behind the counter as though she were talking to someone ill.

Now in a complete daze, the younger woman opened her mouth and spoke. "My name?" She cocked her head slowly to the side, as if she were watching a movie in a different language. "I can't . . ." Just then a short, stout man walked into the room from the back of the cabin. His unlaced boots scuffed the floor loudly as he walked.

"This is worse than we thought, Ulrica," he said loudly in a rough voice. "Are you done mixing?" The woman with the thick braid nodded.

"My name . . ." The younger woman still sat in a trance, trying to remember what would seem to be the most fundamental detail of someone's life.

"Snap out of it!" the short man hollered as he grabbed the woman's free arm.

She screamed and bolted for the exit, knocking over her chair in the process. Ulrica beat her to the door, arms stretched out, ready to catch the would-be escapee. Confused and scared, the woman bent forward and collapsed onto her knees, sobbing. "What do you want from me? Who am I?" she sobbed, holding the child who lay quietly, almost doll-like, in her arms.

"You were too harsh, Bancroft!" Ulrica reprimanded. "You have gone and terrified her. That's no way to win this battle!"

"Oh, so now it's my fault?" Bancroft shouted, throwing his arms into the air in frustration.

"Yes!" she retorted, her anger clearly displayed in her fiery eyes. She walked slowly up to the young woman, her bare feet silent on the wooden floor. As Ulrica bent down, she noticed the woman was whispering prayers in between sobs of anguish. "Poor thing." Ulrica touched the woman's shoulder and knelt down on one knee beside her. Her other hand went to the woman's small chin, lifting her head ever so slowly. "Look into my eyes, dear," she said softly, with power resonating with every word. "Look into my eyes."

The young woman did as she was told and lifted her gaze to Ulrica's dark almond-shaped eyes, immediately catching her breath. She shifted her weight off of her knees and leaned into Ulrica. A sense of calm blanketed her as she let the stranger put her arms around her. Ulrica pushed the woman's wild black locks aside and held her for a moment, rubbing her shoulders and back as a mother would do to soothe a young child. Bancroft faked a cough to catch Ulrica's attention. She looked up at him from the floor, and he tapped his wrist with a thick index finger. Ulrica nodded in affirmation.

"Good," Ulrica whispered to the woman in her arms. The sobbing stopped. "Now, let's go sit down, shall we?"

The younger woman rose to her feet with the help of Ulrica, who assisted her up as she held the baby. Her knees buckled a bit as she took the first step forward. Ulrica kept a guiding arm on her elbow, and Bancroft picked up the fallen chair. He held the chair in place as Ulrica helped lower the woman to her seat.

Bancroft took a seat directly across from the young woman as his wife took the seat next to her. Ulrica held the woman's free hand in her right hand. With her left, she reached into her apron pocket, waited until the young woman's gaze met hers, and then whispered, "Remember." She took her left hand out of her pocket and brought it to her mouth, opened her hand, and softly blew the fine white powder it held into the woman's face. The younger woman inhaled and immediately began coughing, almost choking. She fell out of her chair and onto her back; her head was saved by Ulrica's quick arms. Gasping for air, she turned her head up to the ceiling, letting out a long, suffocated yell as she gasped violently for more breath. She shoved the baby into Ulrica arms and collapsed. "Look,   now you've given her too much!" Bancroft said disapprovingly, with a satisfied grin on his round face.

Ulrica shot her husband a sharp, piercing stare and turned back to the younger woman who was lying in the fetal position, crying softly on the floor. Ulrica carefully held the baby as she sat with her legs crossed before the distraught woman. In the same sugar-sweet voice, she commanded, "Remember. What is your name?"

The younger woman coughed and pushed her black hair out of her face. "I don't remember." She began crying again. Her sobs grew louder as she began losing to the anguish she felt inside.

Sensing her will diminishing, Bancroft came flying around the table, landing on his knees, mere inches from her face. He placed both hands on her and yelled, "REMEMBER, CHILD!" He shook the woman. "YOU MUST REMEMBER! DO IT FOR THE BABY!" With the hands of a lumberjack, he grabbed the woman's head and turned it so the baby could be seen. "WHAT IS YOUR NAME?" he bellowed.

"Dawn," the woman whispered, as she looked into the face of the infant in Ulrica's arms. "My name is Dawn." Immediately, her shaking stopped; she sat up and reached for the chair. Bancroft assisted Dawn to the chair, glancing at his mate in triumph. His blue eyes sparkled as he flashed his white square teeth in a victorious grin.

"You old brute!" Ulrica smiled and rolled her dark eyes as she took the seat next to the battered and dazed younger woman. She gently pushed the baby back into her arms.

"My name is Dawn," the younger woman said again in confirmation, as she readily accepted the bundle.

Bancroft once again took his seat across from the women. He kicked his boots off and stretched his stubby naked toes. "Now, that wasn't so hard, was it?" he chuckled as he pulled a pipe from his jeans and a bag of dried tobacco from his flannel shirt pocket. "Not hard at all."

"What else do you remember?" Ulrica questioned carefully. Her smile had faded. She sat on the edge of her chair, hands folded on her apron. Her thick braid ran straight down her back, the ends of it only inches away from her waist.

"I, I was running. I was scared." Dawn looked into the crevices of the unpolished wooden table as though the table were alive. "I was running, shots were fired, and there were dogs." Her round blue eyes glazed over with fear as she remembered the hounds, the boots, the man who had chased her. "Then I was here." She broke her intense gaze at the table and turned to face the woman sitting beside her. "Who are you?"

"My name is Ulrica," she replied politely, "and *that* over there is my husband, Bancroft." Bancroft rocked back in his chair, scratched his bald head, and chuckled. He wasn't at all fazed by his wife's remarks; in fact, he seemed to enjoy them. He massaged his hairy right foot as he seemingly tried to dissect Dawn with his magnetic blue eyes.

Dawn looked to her left and then to her right at the strangers who offered her shelter. She then centered on the candle in the middle of the table. One candle managed to light the entire cabin. She looked about her, to the worn wooden counter in front of her, to the stove, to the sink with no faucet. There was no other source of light. Dawn focused again on Ulrica, searching her face for an answer. She found it effortless to become lost in every detail. From Ulrica's straight nose to her almond-shaped eyes, she seemed older, but not aged.

"Yes, but *who* are you?"

"Smarter than she looks," huffed Bancroft to himself, clearly entertained.

"We are Beacons." Dawn made no attempt to speak. Bancroft smiled as he noticed a childlike innocence in her eyes. The heavy hand of time had yet to etch itself into her young face. But when he looked beyond the confusion, he saw a sadness in the way the corners of her mouth turned down. He saw a battered body, trying desperately to be strong for the bundle in her arms. "Where do you think you are, young Dawn?"

"I was hoping that you would tell me that I'm dreaming," she replied. There was no smile on her lips; she was serious. Ulrica and Bancroft looked at each other across the table and then simultaneously looked back toward Dawn's insecure face; her delicate features begged to be told a lie. She was so afraid of hearing what she already knew to be true.

"Is there a way back?" Dawn said quietly as she began unraveling a tassel on Josiah's crocheted blanket.

"No," Ulrica said quickly.

"Well," Bancroft corrected her with his eyebrows raised, "there is, but . . ." Ulrica shifted uneasily in her chair and pressed her hands together, uncomfortable with where the discussion was going.

"But what?" Dawn looked up from the blanket and directly at Bancroft, who looked bashfully at his wife and shrugged his shoulders.

"But it's evil," Ulrica broke in, irritated. "You're not evil, are you?"

"No, no, I don't think so." Dawn redirected her gaze to her fingers that were still busy unraveling the tassel. She looked up at Ulrica, her eyes thirsty for comfort. "But how can I know for sure?"

Bancroft emptied the wide bowl of his wooden pipe. "Trust me, darlin'. When you see evil, you will understand."

"What are Beacons? Where am I?" Dawn asked hurriedly. She could sense Ulrica's impatience but needed to satisfy her curiosity.

Ulrica rolled her eyes and crossed her arms, but before she could say anything, her husband spoke.

"You're not in heaven and you're not in hell. You're in the realm in between." Bancroft stood and began to pace the cabin's old wooden floors. He looked rather comical with his loose jean trousers rolled up to the middle of his hairy shins; blue suspenders held up his trousers. Dawn noticed that although he was short and stout, he was not fat. His muscles showed their form through the white T-shirt, and his cotton flannel was unbuttoned and trailed behind him as he strutted back and forth. He had one thick arm behind his back, and the other cradled his short cherry wood pipe. He clearly enjoyed playing teacher, and Dawn made a perfect pupil. "Every being in this realm," he continued as he paced in front of the women, the wooden floor creaking beneath every step, "belongs to one side or the other." He stopped, barefoot, directly in front of Dawn and bent down to meet her, face to face. "If you haven't already noticed," he pointed the curved stem of his pipe at Ulrica and then tapped his own chest with it, "we are good beings."

"How did you get to be here if you're good? Why aren't you in heaven?" Dawn wrestled with reason.

Ulrica stood up from the table. Her long white skirt swished as she moved behind the counter once again. She silently began grinding little yellow seeds to a fine powder. It had been awhile since they had company, and she knew how much Bancroft liked to talk. She remained irritated; they were wasting time with trivial conversation. However, she chose to stay silent. Perhaps it was necessary in some way.

Bancroft took his seat next to Dawn at table. He pulled out his bag of tobacco and began packing the bowl of his pipe again. "We were in Heaven." His movements were slow, and it seemed he had to concentrate and reach far back for this particular memory. "When I would look down onto my people . . . my family," he pulled a splinter off the table and set it in the flame of the candle. "When I saw what burdens I had left them with, not even all the glories of Heaven could comfort me." Bancroft cleared his throat, rubbed his round bald head, and with the splinter aflame, lit his pipe. He took a few puffs, stood up, and began to pace again. Ulrica took a breath and made a motion to speak, but Bancroft exhaled a failed attempt at a smoke ring and began teaching once more.

"I asked around, talked to the authorities, and found there really was such a thing as pure evil. And that not only was my family in danger, but essentially all innocence. So, I volunteered to join the fight . . . the war." He stopped pacing and turned to face Dawn. "I didn't realize then how much of myself I put at stake for this cause. You see, Dawn, there is no afterlife in this realm. You either die forever or get taken prisoner. When the time comes, I pray that they spill my soul and I live on in the memory of my loved ones. There is no coming back from Hell, you know." With that, he sat down and puffed his pipe a number of times until his face was hidden behind a cloud of sweet-smelling smoke. He took a deep satisfied breath and made himself comfortable in the wooden chair.

"So," Dawn began to question.

"Enough about where you are *now*," Ulrica interrupted sharply. There was a bite in her words. "You *need* to remember your past."

"Why is that so important? I'm here now, right?" Dawn looked around, still in disbelief as to where she really was. "I mean, I'm . . . I'm . . . I'm dead." She choked on the last word and struggled to finish her sentence. "So what does it even matter?"

"You look pretty alive to me." Bancroft looked at her.

"But I'm not. You said I died." Dawn knew what she was to believe but fought the facts.

"I don't remember saying that." Bancroft scratched the stubble on his chin in contemplation.

"How do we explain?" Ulrica asked softly as she floated to Dawn's side from behind the counter. She took the vacant seat next to Dawn, reached over, and took Dawn's right hand into her firm grip. "Your body died. Yes." She gently stroked the back of Dawn's soft hand. "Even you remember this, but your soul is still very much alive."

"You're holding my hand," Dawn pointed out and shook her

head "I'm trying to understand, but isn't my hand part of my body?"

Ulrica flashed an agitated glance over to Bancroft and pressed her perfect lips together. Dawn looked to Bancroft and raised a suspecting eyebrow. It seemed as though the couple had exchanged words. Ulrica looked back into Dawn's eyes with fierce intent. "We don't have time to explain this, Dawn."

The sudden change in tone and the fiery look in Ulrica's eyes scared Dawn. She struggled to take her hand back, which proved difficult with Josiah cradled in her other arm. She was unnerved by the hunger growing in Ulrica's eyes. Her small, delicate hand had a firm grip. Dawn felt weak and trapped. She turned her head to look at Bancroft. Ulrica grabbed her by the chin with her other hand and stared into Dawn's face as she kept talking. Her words seemed to echo from her slender frame.

"Your body died but your soul kept running. Had you stayed by your body, you wouldn't be here. An angel would have come for your soul. But you kept running." Ulrica's grip was getting tighter, and Dawn became more frightened. It seemed as though this woman had the strength of a beast. "This, your hand, is just a shell. Without it your soul would disperse." Bancroft was now standing behind Dawn.

Dawn panicked. She wanted to scream and fight and run. Her mind shot to Josiah in the blanket in her arm. He was so quiet, so still. Bancroft leaned over Dawn and placed both hands on her pale forearm, keeping it flat against the table. With a metallic cling, Ulrica took a dagger with a fat blade and a bone handle from behind her back.

"What, what are you doing?" Dawn was frantic. Her legs flailed underneath the table. "Stop! I, I understand! Don't do this!"

"Your soul is what keeps you alive," Ulrica's voice bellowed inside the cabin walls. "Your body was just that, a vessel, just like this shell." With one quick movement she slashed Dawn's wrist. Dawn screamed in pain and then watched in astonishment as a liquid silver type substance came trickling out of the cut. Dawn stopped screaming and watched as this weightless bluish-silver liquid flowed upward, and from her body.

"What . . . is . . . that?" Dawn was mesmerized as the liquid formed bubbles in midair, weightless.

"That is your soul," Ulrica replied, no longer looking wild, no longer pinning Dawn's arm down. Dawn raised her free hand to touch the liquid, but before she could, Ulrica took her wrist and brought it in contact with the floating liquid. To Dawn's amazement, the liquid merged to her wound. The smaller drops seemed attracted to the bigger ones and to the cut itself. Dawn watched as Ulrica guided the rest of the soul back into her body. She watched with an open mouth as Ulrica held the wound tight, careful not to let out anymore of the beautiful thick liquid. Ulrica reached into her apron pocket, produced a pale-green putty, and began rubbing it into the slit on Dawn's wrist, carefully trapping all of the soul. Dawn took her hand back after watching Ulrica close the wound.

"Your soul," Bancroft finished. "Do you believe us now?" Bancroft stood behind his wife with his hands on her shoulders.

"Do I have a choice?" Dawn said as she looked at the pair, sober from the incident and still rubbing her scar. "What about Joey? Is he?"

"Yes," Ulrica said, forcing out a small smile. "You need to remember more from your former life. Your soul was not a healthy color."

"What do you mean? It was beautiful."

"It was too silver," said Bancroft, shaking his head. "Not enough blue. You don't have much time."

Dawn sighed, annoyed by the onset of more mystery. "Time for . . . ?"

"If you don't remember soon, you will become a sliver." Ulrica tried to say this gently, but the last word came out harsh, cold.

"A sliver?" Dawn looked at the two, and her brow creased with lines of frustration. "Look, you guys. If I try my damnedest to give you the answers you want, will you at least meet me halfway? Shells, slivers, and all your powder is really," she huffed, staring at the fresh wound, "incredibly overwhelming." She had no intention of being rude. But she had, after all, died today. She had a crazed hunger for answers, but more than anything, she wanted to lose the fear.

Ulrica and Bancroft smiled. "Deal," they said together.

Ulrica continued. "A sliver is what you would call a ghost."

"But I'm already here in a shell," Dawn interrupted.

"Let me just continue," Ulrica said, slightly annoyed. "It will go much faster this way." Dawn nodded apologetically as she shifted in her chair. "Your soul can transform when it reaches certain stages. Your shell will become weak and malleable. Your conscience is what keeps your soul together. Well, that and your shell. If you cannot remember your past, you will slowly begin to lose your conscience. No one can live without one, whether it be good or bad."

Ulrica gave Dawn a second to digest the information. She couldn't help but think how helpless and vulnerable the young woman looked sitting there, infant in arm. "You see," she continued, "without your memories, you will become a sliver. Parts of your soul are already making that transformation." She looked up at her husband, who was still standing behind her. "We saw it ourselves; there was hardly any blue. That is not a sign of a healthy soul."

Dawn rubbed the green putty on her wrist and looked at the couple solemnly. "Can you come back from being a sliver?"

"No one ever has," said Bancroft sadly. "You need to remember, dear." He left his wife's side and went to help Dawn out of her chair. Dawn allowed Bancroft to lead her to the back of the cabin. "Perhaps a nap will help you remember."

Bancroft held Dawn by her elbow and led her past the wall that held the stove and cabinets. At the very back of the cabin, behind the wall, was a short flight of creaky, uneven wooden stairs. At the bottom of the steps, the pair took an immediate right and entered a small room. Dawn had to duck her head as she entered to not hit the wooden door frame. Once inside, she straightened her back and could feel the hairs on top of her head graze the ceiling. Roots poked out of the walls, and the whole room smelled of earth. Rich, dark earth. High in the right-hand corner of the room, there was a tiny rectangular window that provided no light. Nothing adorned the walls. There was no closet and no other doors, just what looked to be a full-sized bed and an extremely unstable nightstand that held a solitary candle in its center. The bed looked cozy and warm, and even though Dawn had never slept in it, she looked forward to the comfort she knew it would provide.

Bancroft gestured forward with one arm and then turned and walked out of the room. Dawn could hear the wooden boards creak as he made his way back upstairs to his beautiful wife. She turned, sighed, and laid herself down above the covers, fully clothed. Holding Josiah in her arms, she began to ponder the events of the day.

She whispered to Josiah, "Maybe when we close our eyes we will wake up and this will all just be a bad dream." She sighed and held his big round baby head in her hand as she leaned in to kiss his velvety skin. She frowned, knowing this was no dream.

Suddenly and without caution, the door swung open; Ulrica was standing in the doorway. Her hair was wild, and she wore a dangerous smile. Dawn knew she was up to something, but before she could react, Ulrica laughed and pulled her slender hand out of her apron pocket. With a deep breath, she blew a cloud of white powder so large that the entire room looked foggy. Dawn just moaned and laid her head back on her pillow. No use fighting it. She closed her eyes and began to drift. When she realized she had forgotten something, she peeked at the baby. "I love you, Joey." Dawn kissed him gently on his button nose. Josiah seemed so calm, almost like he knew everything was going to be all right. He lifted his little curled fist to a lock of her black hair, wrapped his fat fingers around it, and tugged gently. Then they both fell into a deep sleep.

The dreams were of the past.

---- Chapter 3 ----
The Past

"If thou shalt seek the Lord, thou shalt find Him." Dawn loved her pastor. Some in the congregation thought he was too young.

"How much can such a young man know about life?" the elders would say from the pew, shaking their heads. Yet, despite their discontent, they all came back week after week to hear the words of their young pastor. Dawn belonged to the part of the congregation that believed his messages where more important than his age. She found strength and faith in his words every Sunday. She believed the young, blond-haired pastor thoroughly understood what it meant to be Christian, but also understood what it meant to be human. He was a rarity and a blessing. She trusted him. That's why every Sunday she sat in the fourth pew on the right, next to her mother, who also loved, trusted, and respected the pastor and his preaching. Dawn was not a very religious person and had only her mother to thank for finally coming to know God. "The Lord knows we all need some Good News in our lives." He finished the sermon, bowed his head, and the congregation read the Lord's Prayer together before going home.

When he hit, he hit hard. He knew better than to hit her face. He used her body for a punching bag. One hit after the other, until sweat beads dripped off his nose.

"If yew eva," he said with another swift kick to her stomach, "eva lie to me again . . ." He came down on one knee to meet her on the floor, and with his rough hand pushed her hair, wet with tears, off her face. He looked deep into her scared eyes. ". . . I swear to yew..." His red hair was wet with sweat and laid heavy on his head and his green eyes searched her face for another reason to hit her. Dawn lay paralyzed, afraid to move, afraid to breathe, silently praying for the beating to be over with. He grabbed her hair into a tight fist and pressed her head deep into the carpet, "I'll kill ya!"

He caressed her face and kissed her gently on the forehead before getting up. He towered over her crippled body, watching her for a few seconds. She knew better than to speak. She knew better than to whine or sniffle.

Just lie still, she told herself. *You did a great job. He will be gone in a minute.*

While putting on his jean jacket, he checked his square face in the mirror and ran his fingers through his damp crimson hair. He turned as he reached for the doorknob.

"When I get back, this mess better be cleaned up." He opened the door and closed it silently behind him. Dawn lay soundless on the carpet as she listened to his heavy boots make their way down the porch steps. She lay dormant and waited to hear him fire up the engine to his black, souped-up, '64 Chevy Short Bed. She stayed still until she could no longer hear the pounding of his muffler. Once everything was quiet, she took a deep breath and yowled in pain. She rolled into the fetal position, hands holding her ribs. Through stifling sobs, she began to search for her phone. It lay only two feet away from her on the carpet, next to the broken coffee table.

Reaching for the phone was almost as painful as the beating itself. *It would be easier to die* she thought as she stretched her right arm over her head. Her forearm cracked loudly as her fingers used the loops in the carpet to creep her body closer. She screamed in agony. With a broken arm, she managed to grab the phone and pull it close to her. She paused for a moment before dialing.

"If yew ever call the police, I'll kill yew!" She heard his words as though he were right there, spitting them in her face.

"I wish you would," she whispered before dialing 9-1-1.

This was the first time Dawn had ever called 9-1-1. As she lay there in a pool of tears, waiting for the ambulance to come, she wondered what had ever taken her so long.

She opened her eyes and winced in pain. Her hand squeezed another. She looked down to see her mother's sleeping face resting on her lap. She marveled at how young she still looked. The crow's feet at the corners of her eyes were proof of how much she loved to smile and laugh. Dawn remembered that the frown lines and the wrinkles in the brow came only after her father passed away. Looking at her mother, Dawn realized it was almost impossible to tell her age. Only the grey in her wavy black hair revealed the truth.

She wanted to reach out and run her fingers through her mother's hair. Dawn cringed as a shockwave of pain ran through her right arm. She looked down and realized her arm was in a cast. It was then that Dawn remembered the beating, the phone call. She frantically looked around her hospital room, remembering the threats, half expecting to see him standing at the foot of the bed with that murderous look he got when she really crossed him. To her relief, the room was empty. To her right was a vacant bed, freshly prepped and waiting for the next patient. There were two faded-yellow chairs in the corner that looked old and abandoned. Even the walls were empty. There was only one picture on the pale-yellow walls; it was of Jesus. She stared at Him for a long time. He looked so clean and innocent. His brown wavy hair hung over his left shoulder. His head tilted upward toward a light. *What is he looking at?* Dawn wondered before she dropped her gaze and looked about the room. She was not surprised that there were no cards, no flowers—just her mother sitting in a chair, her head resting on Dawn's lap. *I wonder how long she has been here holding my hand?* With that thought, she squeezed her mother's hand tightly.

"Mom," she whispered.

Her mother awoke, rubbing the sleep lines from the side of her face.

"How are you feeling, sweetheart?" Her voice was soft—the softest voice Dawn had ever heard from the only real friend Dawn had ever known. Her mother was the only friend Tucker, Dawn's husband, allowed her to have. "I wish your father were here," her mother said sharply, raising her hand to caress daughter's face. "He'd take care of him."

A knock at the door made both of their hearts skip with fear. The door slowly crept open, and a young doctor popped his shaggy head in. The women exhaled and smiled as the doctor walked in.

He strolled up to the bed, clipboard in arm. "Miss Chitoe?"

"Please, call me Dawn," she managed to whisper.

"My name is Dr. Reed. You were in pretty bad shape when the emergency team brought you in. You have a broken ulna. That's one of the bones in your forearm," he added after both women looked confused. They simultaneously looked at the arm in a cast and then back up to the doctor. "You have a number of fractured ribs as well. That's why your breathing is difficult. Your other injuries were minor, which, judging from your bruises, is actually a blessing." He smiled a nervous smile before glancing back down to the clipboard.

"I know you must be in an awful amount of pain. And we will give you more pain medication, if you wish." He hugged his clipboard and pressed his lips together before exhaling through flared nostrils. "However, you need to know that since you are pregnant, the less pain medication we give you, the better it will be for your baby."

"When God closes one door, another one opens. All in agreement, say amen."

Pregnancy was fun for Dawn. She transformed her extra bedroom into a nursery. She painted the walls bright yellow and the borders light green. Her mother bought her a mahogany crib and a jungle-themed crib set. When money allowed, Dawn bought stuffed baby animals and soft, plush, pastel blankets. What she enjoyed most about the pregnancy was that it was Tucker-free. After a few weeks in prison and finding out about the pregnancy, he wanted nothing more to do with Dawn.

She turned around, smiling after hanging a cloud, sun, and moon mobile on the side of the crib. She happily wiped her hands on her yellow sundress with satisfaction on finishing another project. Her calico cat meowed by her bare feet; she carefully bent over and picked him up.

"I feel like my life is finally turning around, Jimmy Bean," she whispered into the scruff of the cat's neck. He pawed playfully at her banana-shaped earrings before she bent over to put him back on the nursery floor.

"Ughh," she grunted as she tried to push herself back to her feet. Ughh," she said as she collapsed onto her knees. It felt as though someone had punched her in the stomach, and in an instant, a stomach cramp brought her down onto the floor. She felt the inside of her thighs grow warm. She brought her shaking hands to her face and screamed when she saw they were covered in blood. She knew she was going to lose the baby.

The night sky was clear. Dawn felt like she could see every star in the sky as she lay in her wooden lawn chair. It was all so beautiful—the stars, the moon so big she felt she could reach up and grab it. Her mother's words rang clear in her head:. "God made you this beautiful world, and all you can do is sit around and mope all day." She adjusted the pillow beneath her head as she tried to appreciate the scene. The grass was long in her backyard. When the welcomed breeze blew, it wisped the grass back and forth. The crickets and grasshoppers seemed to be singing her a sweet summer lullaby. *God really did do a good job creating this earth* she thought, trying to be grateful. Her hands made their way down to her belly and rested there for a fraction of a second. She quickly took them off and jerked up out of her seat, letting the small pillow fall to the ground.

"If only he'd care this much about all his creations," she said as she took one last look at the stars. They seemed to be mocking her, teasing her as they twinkled. She dropped her head, picked up the fallen pillow, and went inside.

All of the windows were open, and her home was rich with the scents of a cool spring evening. Jimmy Bean came up and rubbed his side against her ankles, but she ignored him. He stretched and took a seat in front of her on the living room carpet, not far from where she called 9-1-1. Watching her, waiting for her to reach down and stroke his back the way she always had.

Dawn stood, facing the mirror that hung on the wall, staring at her reflection. She wondered what could have been if she hadn't had such a weak body. If she hadn't had that stillbirth. She began hearing crying baby noises.

"No," Dawn whispered as she held her hands to her ears. "No, no, no, no." She ran to the kitchen to get her medication as the crying got louder. *It sounds so real,* she thought.

"Why are you doing this to me?" she screamed with her head tilted toward the ceiling. "Why? I do everything right! I haven't done anything to deserve this! Wasn't it enough for you to take him?" She swallowed her pills without water, and the baby's cries continued. "Why?" she sobbed. The crying was so real, she felt as though she could touch the sound. She covered her ears again and closed her eyes. She rested her head in her hands as she dug her elbows into the kitchen counter, praying the cries would dissipate and take her memories with them. When she lifted her head, she found herself staring directly at the set of knives that were stored neatly in their wooden holder. She looked at them almost longingly and then pushed them violently aside. The knives went crashing onto the kitchen floor. The crying stopped. She turned, leaned against the counter, and then slid her back down until she was sitting on the floor, holding her knees to her chest, sobbing, wetting her jeans with her tears.

Jimmy Bean was at the front door now, meowing and pawing at the beige carpet in front of it.

He probably wants to leave me too, she thought. *Hell, I want to leave me.* She pulled herself to her feet and walked through the small living room. She kept her head down as she passed the mirror so as not to catch a glimpse of herself. She turned the knob on her front door and let the cat out. He didn't bolt like he usually did and this stopped Dawn from closing the door behind him.

She opened the door to see what had caught his attention.

The cat was sniffing a naked baby! There was a naked baby on her front porch!

"Well, that settles it! I'm committing myself!" she said out loud. She went to close the door; the baby made a happy gurgling sound as the cat sniffed him and prodded him with his paw. "Are you real?" Dawn whispered, questioning her sanity as she knelt down.

Sitting outside in her favorite patio chair, she rocked the baby to and fro. He was wrapped snuggly in a crotched blanket his grandmother had knit him. Dawn sang to the baby, which was something she didn't do well, but he didn't seem to mind. His big blue eyes laughed at her when she missed the notes.

He had one pudgy little hand wrapped tightly around her pinky and the other around her heart. She laughed at his little round face when he blew bubbles or smiled his toothless smile. She felt that she could hold him forever. Dawn looked into the night. No stars, no crickets, no moon. Just night. She thanked God and said a prayer.

Dawn named him Josiah. Only one person knew that he wasn't her baby, and her mother was much too in love to tell anyone the truth.

"Didn't I tell you God is good?" she said. Her brown eyes wrinkled deep at the corners as she focused only on Josiah. "Didn't I tell you?" she chuckled.

"I got my rights, Dawn!" His country drawl repulsed her.

"What rights, Tucker?" she huffed, handing Josiah over to her mother, who was horrified at the idea of sharing Josiah with another, with a monster.

"You beat me and left me to die while I was pregnant! Or don't you remember that?" Dawn yelled into the phone. She felt a sense of power. It was unreal to her, for she had never raised her voice to him before.

"I got a right to see my child!" Tucker's anger was growing. Dawn remembered him. Dawn feared him. She feared his strength and how dangerously unstable he was. But mostly, Dawn feared his ability to always get what he wanted. "I'm comin' tamarro."

Dawn knew by the tone of his voice that he would be there in the morning. This was no idle threat; this was a fact. Panic began to overwhelm her. The new sense of power she felt coursing through her veins was fleeting. She knew he'd come, and she knew that if he chose to, he would take Josiah with him when he left. She would be powerless to stop him. No matter how hard she would fight him, he would get what he wanted. She could not let that happen.

"No, Tucker!" she yelled into the phone. "He's not your child." After the words left her lips, she immediately wished she could retract them.

"Wha' now?" he asked. She knew he was thinking, she knew he sat there with his forehead lines burrowing deep into his skull. She knew he would catch her fatal slip of words before she could even try to back out of them. He began to chuckle, but it wasn't a friendly chuckle, it was a deadly one.

"Yew, yew cheated on me?"

Dawn, with the phone still to her ear, was already upstairs packing her things. She grabbed the faded photograph of her and her father, taken so many years back when things were simple. "Bait the hook, throw it in, and wait, darlin'," he would say. "If they bite, you win. If not, there's always tomorrow." But there isn't. You are guaranteed nothing. And Dawn knew this better than most. She grabbed the wooden jewelry box her mom had made for her. The few items that meant the most to her barely filled the small travel bag. She hurriedly made her way back down the steps to find that her mother had put the baby down on the couch. She was in the kitchen, busy packing her oversized purse with bottles and formula.

"He won't get the baby, Dawn," she whispered as she picked nipples out of the bottle sanitizer. "I'll make sure of it." Her wrinkled hands trembled as she threw anything they might need into the bag.

"YEW BITCH!" Tucker started on the other end of the phone. Dawn flinched. She knew if he had been there, there would have been a fist to go along with those words. "I'M GONNA KILL YOU AND YOUR BABY. YOU DON'T DESERVE TO LIVE!" She shook with fear as she ran down the porch steps, her bag in one arm, the cat in the other. She didn't bother locking the door; Tucker was going to kick it down anyway.

Her mother snapped the buckle over Josiah's chest and jumped into the driver's side.

"Hang up," she mouthed to her daughter, who was buckling herself in.

Tucker was screaming obscenities into her ear, and behind his growling voice, she could hear his truck engine roar to life. She hung up the phone.

"MA, GO! GO NOW!" she yelled in panic. "PLEASE HURRY!" Dawn's mother didn't need to hear that twice. She cranked the engine to her Buick station wagon and took off, leaving a cloud of orange dust behind them. "He's gonna kill me!" Dawn said to herself out loud. "He's gonna kill me!"

Her mother drove like a bat out of hell.

"MOM!" Dawn fell to her knees in front of the bloodied body of her lifeless mother. Blood covered her mother's entire shirt, and her body was still warm. With Josiah in one arm and her mother's limp body in the other, Dawn lifted her face and screamed, "It's all my fault! It's all my fault. Why have I been forsaken?" Then she whispered into her mother's ear, "Please forgive me, please forgive me."

She ran out the cabin door with the baby wrapped in his blanket, held tightly to her chest. Dawn made a mad dash for the forest behind her great-uncle's cabin. She tore through the thick underbelly of the forest, knowing she would not be able to outrun them forever.

"DAWN!" Tucker yelled through the trees. "Did you see what I did to your mom?" He chuckled, relishing what he had done. She screamed in anguish as she pictured her mother lying in a pool of blood. She kept running, knowing he was only moments behind her. Shots were fired; each time they sounded closer. Josiah was so silent and still in her arms. She clutched him closer as she hurdled a fallen tree. It was then that Dawn reached a clearing. She paused, looking back only to see a massive figure forcing his way through the woods. She dashed into the field that quickly turned to marsh. He was right behind her now. She was knee-deep in the swampy waters, pulling at her cargo pants, looking into the twin barrels of his shotgun. "You and your bastard child can go to hell!" His green eyes were red with fury. He pulled the trigger.

With a bang, she woke up to find herself covered in sweat. Josiah was awake lying quietly beside her.

The tears were still spilling down her face as she looked about the room, terrified by the memories. Silently, another feeling came upon her. As the last of her silver tears ran off her chin, the hairs on the back of her neck began to rise. She was being watched. She was being hunted. She knew she wasn't alone.

A shadow crossed the room, and with a start, she turned to see what was at the cellar window, but she was too slow. All at once, there were erratic rustling sounds outside of the basement window, accompanied by husky breathing. Whatever it was, she knew there was more than one.

Dawn slowly bent over to pick up Josiah and then quietly lifted herself off the bed so as to not make a sound. The snarling grew louder as she clutched Joey to her chest. Keeping her eyes on the window, she began to back her way to the door. The scratching was getting louder; they were trying to dig their way in. The more they dug, the faster they dug.

A loud thud made Dawn want to yelp, but a quick and firm hand covered her mouth. This only terrified her more, causing her heart to prance violently inside her chest. That's when she saw it staring at her through the window. A beast so hideous that if her mouth weren't already covered, she would have screamed. Slowly, she felt herself being pulled back through the door. She let her body be guided, sure that whatever was pulling her was more pleasant than what was still staring at her through the small cellar window. Its yellow demon-like eyes seemed to pierce through her very existence. The beast resembled a wolf with long, sharp claws, but no wolf she had ever seen had a snout that long with that many jagged teeth. Its fur was matted and dreadlocked. What caught her attention more than anything else was the way it held its stare. Long, hard, she felt it knew what she was thinking. Before Bancroft closed the door, she saw the beast smirk and say, "I am watching you."

Chapter 4

Afraid of the Dark

O nce the wooden cellar door was firmly shut, Bancroft pushed Dawn, with Josiah in her arms, up the creaky wooden stairs. He left her at the top of the steps and ran back down into the cellar. The room she knew to be the living area was dark and cold. Only short hours ago it was warm and full of light and comfort. Dawn shivered as she heard a huff in the darkness.

"Bancroft . . . Ulrica?" She squinted into the black and strained her ears. Again, she heard a single huff. The floorboard creaked, and she knew she was not alone in that little room. Keeping her blind eyes on the dark void in front of her, she began to back up.

"Who's there?" Her question was a scared whisper.

CRACK! Dawn's body seized in fear, and then there was light. Ulrica stood directly in front of her, holding a flame in between her thumb and slender middle finger. *Had she been that close the whole time?* Dawn thought. The flame was so close to Dawn's face she could feel the heat lick the bridge of her nose. Ulrica stood like a statue in front of her. Her face was taut and her strong jaw was clenched. The flame was only bright enough to illuminate their faces. Dawn didn't have to see the rest of Ulrica to know that her hair was standing on end. There was something about Ulrica's deep black eyes that seemed to breach her inner being.

"I'm watching you."

Dawn shivered again as a tear streamed down her face, leaving a sparkling silver line in its trail.

"What is going on?" Dawn whispered as her eyes searched

Ulrica's. Ulrica didn't answer. Ulrica turned with the flame still in between her fingers and walked to the humble table in the middle of the room, her bare feet silent on the wooden boards. She bent over and lit the candle in the center of the table; it was as though Ulrica simply dropped the flame in its place. Like before, the small candle managed to fill most of the room, instantly forming a more welcoming atmosphere. Ulrica walked behind her island, untied her frazzled hair, and began running her fingers through the long black mane. Within a few seconds, her hair began to look like black silk flowing through her gentle fingers. Her eyes seemed to be losing that savage glare; it seemed as though the danger had passed.

"What is going on?" Dawn repeated angrily, standing with her back straight as she held Josiah. "Tell me!" she demanded.

Ulrica, whose hair was now hanging over her shoulder in a thick braid, placed both hands on the countertop and leaned forward.

"Do you consider yourself a girl or a woman?" she asked. A playful smile danced on her full lips. "Are you anymore grown than that babe in your arms?"

"What the hell are you talking about?" Dawn felt offended and patronized. Her anger began to grow deep within her, but her fear still kept her frozen in place.

With banging, heavy steps, Bancroft made his way up the stairs and past Dawn, who was standing in the same spot where he had left her minutes before. Dawn watched as he took a seat at the table. She wasn't sure, but it seemed as if the flame of the candle had grown brighter with his arrival. She stood blinking at the edge of the steps, not exactly sure what to do with herself.

"The Gidlies never come this close," Bancroft said, but not to Dawn, as he shook his head in disbelief. "Never."

Ulrica smiled from behind the counter. Her movements were exact, yet graceful. Still and quiet, she prepared a pink elixir, a spoon of that and a dab of this. The clinking of her beaded turquoise bracelet was the only sound that came from her. She seemed content, almost happy, as she plucked the petals off of a red flower and added them to her mixture.

"He saw us." Bancroft spoke more to himself than to any one particular person. He reached his hand into his jeans pocket and pulled out his polished pipe. With his other hand, he reached into his flannel lumberjack shirt pocket and took out his smoke. He did this with such familiarity; Dawn figured it came from spending a lifetime in the same clothes.

"He knows we are here," Bancroft continued, as he packed his pipe with perfection. He looked up to his wife, who was still diligently working, calmly measuring and decisively scooping.

"Tomorrow we leave, come sunrise we go." And with those last words he lit and puffed heavily on his pipe.

Dawn watched the two silently. She still hadn't moved. She was silently praying she would wake up and find that it was all just a bad dream. She imagined walking down the stairs of her old home. Her mother would be waiting for her at the bottom with a cup of coffee in her favorite cat-shaped cup. She would tell her mom all about her dream. She could see her mom running to the bookshelf, excited and smiling, reaching for the dream dictionary. She envisioned the two of them sitting on the couch, coffee cups in hand, laughing at her sick mind, finding an explanation to all of the things she remembered from her horrible dream. She remembered the way her mom laughed, her beautiful mother, her wonderful life.

As she stood, only feet away from the stairs, she looked around the cabin. She looked at Bancroft, his back turned to her as he sat with his elbows on the table. Through his billows of smoke, Dawn looked at Ulrica. Just looking at her made her feel cold and alone. Everything was so foreign. What had she ever done to deserve this? Everything had been taken from her. *Why?* she thought as she looked up. Tears were beginning to flood her vision. She felt like crying, like falling onto her knees and wailing. But Josiah beat her to the punch and broke the silence.

That was the first time Dawn had heard Josiah make any sound since they had arrived. His cry didn't bother her. In fact, she didn't even try to soothe his yell. She let him cry; she held her head back, eyes closed, and let him scream. She stood there, smiling, as she listened to the sound of his voice. *Oh, how I've missed this!* Josiah's face reddened with every jagged breath he took. His fists pumped with aggravation. Dawn held her head back in exaltation. *Finally someone's voice was being heard.* Her ears drank up his intense cries. For a moment, she felt at peace.

"Er . . ." Bancroft turned in his seat to look behind him and gave her a worried look.

Dawn opened her eyes. Her cheeks flushed red when she noticed she was the center of attention.

"Oh, sorry," Dawn whispered bashfully. "It's just that I hadn't heard Joey cry since the . . . the incident. I thought maybe something was wrong with him."

She looked down at the bundle in her arms, giving the baby her full attention. Her beautiful hair rippled over her soft shoulders as she began to rock him side to side.

"Shhhh, hush now," she whispered gently as she stroked his chubby red cheeks with her index finger. "Everything is going to be okay." Josiah instantly stopped crying and went into a whimper. He reached his fat baby hand up and grabbed one of her dark spiraling curls, gently tugging it. "That's your favorite one, isn't it?" Dawn gently kissed him on his forehead. She smiled as his sniffles faded and she began to make her way to the table.

"Bancroft," Dawn spoke as she pulled out a chair next to his, "what's a Gidly?"

Bancroft huffed, slightly taken aback by the sudden change of topic. "It's bad news, that's what it is!"

Ulrica looked over to her frazzled husband, smiled sweetly, and continued chopping and sorting and bottling. She now worked on a purple powder, effortlessly grinding leaves and flower petals together, producing a fine dust.

"Oh, my love, you're always so emotional," she said, looking Dawn directly in her eyes. "Gidlies," she began softly, "are insatiable creatures. They are normally used by demons as a type of bounty hunter. They, like bloodhounds, have an absolutely flawless sense of smell and an unmistakable howl."

"What brought them here?" Dawn asked under her breath. She already knew the answer to her question. Ulrica continued looking at her with a stern, all-knowing stare.

Dawn's eyes grew wide with amazement as she noticed that although Ulrica's eyes were planted firmly on her, her hands were still busy sifting and bottling. Ulrica let a satisfied grin crack her lips and continued speaking, not once looking down.

"These beings patrol *their* side of this world. They are foot soldiers, like us." She looked over at her husband who was silently puffing his pipe with his elbows planted on the table, back humped, deep in thought. "They fight for their side, like us. They are known for their ruthless ways, like . . ."

"Evil ways," grumbled Bancroft through a plume of smoke.

Dawn listened as she watched Ulrica's magic hands. She looked up, expecting to see Ulrica's piercing eyes, and was comforted to see that Ulrica was once again immersed in the mixtures on her table.

Ulrica continued, paying no attention to Dawn. "Gidlies can take two forms: an animal form, which you witnessed just now, and their normal human form. They usually only take their animal form when they are fighting or hunting."

"They can be *any* animal at *any* time?" Dawn broke in with a hint of distress in her voice.

"No, dear," Ulrica continued gently. "They can choose what they want to be as long as it's around the same size as their natural selves."

"That's why the wolves are so big," Dawn said matter-of-factly, staring at the wall, remembering the large beast with saliva dripping from its teeth "I'm watching you." She shivered and snapped her attention back to Ulrica, who was still working on her potions, ever the humble scientist.

"Ulrica," Dawn hesitated, "can they be *any* creature? I mean, if the size allows?"

"Yes. Airborne, water, or land. The transformation hurts and takes some energy from them, so don't change on a daily basis. However, just because one chooses to be a bird, it does not mean he can fly. "

Dawn sat quietly for a moment, digesting this new information. She had so many questions and had to make a real effort to only ask the important ones. "How do you know it's a Gidly and not some other creature?"

"Well, usually their yellow eyes and their ferociousness give them away," Ulrica said, throwing a quick glance over to her husband who still hadn't moved.

Dawn caught Ulrica's glance and asked before thinking, "I don't understand. Why is Bancroft so upset?"

Bancroft shot Dawn an impatient look, but Ulrica's tongue was faster to speak than his.

"Because, dear. Bancroft," she stared into his round, watered eyes and continued her explanation, "has seen what true evil Gidlies are capable of. He has seen what they can do to one's soul. He has seen them in action. They are most unforgiving."

Dawn was beginning to understand, but questions still loomed above her.

"Why do they have these powers? Where do you get powers like that? Do I have any powers?"

"Dawn, understand this." Ulrica stopped working, wiped her hands, and came from behind the counter. Her long white skirt flowed with her slender frame, and her beaded belt clinked softly as she stopped in front of Dawn. Dawn moved uneasily in her chair, too timid to look Ulrica in the face. She would rather not be this close to her. Ulrica bent down on one knee. Her presence commanded Dawn to look at her.

"Beings with abilities usually had to give up something for them. The Devil and some demons can give beings powers for very heavy prices. This makes any evil being with powers even more dangerous."

"Selling your soul," Dawn whispered, as Ulrica rose and walked over to Bancroft. She gently massaged his broad shoulders before planting a kiss on the top of his bald head and silently made her way back to her place behind the counter.

"Does that mean no good beings have powers?" Dawn questioned after some silent moments of thought. "That sounds pretty unfair."

Ulrica shot Dawn another impatient look, reminding Dawn of one of her high school teachers who always seemed annoyed by the voice of his students. Dawn understood. No more questions.

She bowed her head and looked at Josiah. He was fast asleep in her arms; his tiny fist still held her curl. He looked so peaceful. Dawn wondered what his dreams were made of as she played with the small tuft of blonde hair on his head and stroked his round cheeks with her index finger. She lifted Josiah closer to her face, dug her nose into his neck, and breathed him in. He still smelled the same. *Like candy and kittens.* Dawn smiled to herself, and after another whiff, wondered if she was simply imagining or somehow remembering his scent. Was it really possible? Can your scent follow you after death and into the afterlife?

"Some of us have powers," Bancroft grumbled, seemingly to himself. "They are hard to come by because they have to be given to you. By God or an angel, but since angels aren't allowed down here . . . powers are scarce."

Dawn took a breath to ask a question. Ulrica interrupted.

"No more talk now. Let us prepare for our departure. There is a lot to do and precious little time to do it in."

Dawn had the impression that Ulrica did not want her knowing too much. Was it for her own protection? Or was it simply because there were too many questions that needed answering? Perhaps some questions were best answered through one's own adventures.

Morning soon came. No one rested much; no one spoke much. Dawn sat holding Josiah, humming and rocking. He giggled some, yawned some, slept some, but never cried. He was so content in Dawn's arms. The others noticed this, and when they weren't busy getting ready, they would stop by and wiggle a finger or gently kiss his bare feet. Apparently, the way one treats a baby in the afterlife isn't at all different from how one treats a baby in the earthly life.

Dawn was not sure what lie ahead of her. She only knew that she felt at ease when she had Josiah cuddled to her bosom. In a funny way, she felt as though maybe there was a connection between the two of them. As he curled his fingers around her lock of hair, its ends tickled his nose and they both smiled.

"I love you so much," Dawn whispered into his ear and planted a kiss right above it. She still had trouble understanding how one could smell the same, look the same, smile the same, but not be the same. She tried not to dwell on that thought or any of the other hundreds of thoughts that were racing through her mind.

She watched the others as they prepared. A couple of times she offered her help; each time her help was rejected. She did not really mind; she was only asking to be polite.

Bancroft spent the night cleaning and brandishing weapons of different sizes and shapes. Sometimes he would stand up and wield a weapon. Dawn would watch, amazed at how smooth his movements were for his age and stature. He smiled as he held the short ax in his hand, weighed it, checked its balance, and then within the blink of an eye, twirled it, flipped it, and caught it in his other hand. Satisfied with his performance, he bowed to himself and went on inspecting the next weapon in line.

Ulrica hadn't moved much from her station. She had sorted and mixed and ground and mixed and sorted some more. When she worked, she never made a sound, she never complained about her tedious work, and she never looked up. She seemed content in her duties. By daybreak, Ulrica was placing small sacks and vials in three brown satchels that lay by the foot of the door. As she stood and looked out of the window, the rising sun shone directly on her face. Dawn marveled at her almost perfect features. Ulrica's skin was sun kissed and lacked any imperfections; the sun blotted out the few wrinkles that she had. Her black hair was shiny and long as it hung over her shoulder. Dawn could only marvel at how beautiful Ulrica was. Dawn knew she was older, but she could not tell how much older. She began to wonder if Ulrica only seemed older because of her maturity and not because of her actual age. Dawn looked back down at Josiah and pondered what age actually was. She began questioning if time even mattered here.

"It is time," Ulrica said quietly, simultaneously answering Dawn's thoughts and handing a satchel to Bancroft before turning to Dawn.

"Your arm must be getting tired, my dear," she said, as she began wrapping a long, tan, woven scarf around Dawn, tying Josiah tightly to her chest. "There, that should hold him. Now your arms will be free." Ulrica then quickly braided her hair and threw her own satchel over her shoulders. Bancroft stepped forward and handed Ulrica two small tomahawks.

"My weapons of choice." Ulrica smiled as she admired their aged wooden handles. The curved handles fit most perfectly in her delicate hands. She kissed the heads of each before sliding them in between her tan beaded belt and cotton skirt.

"You might need this." Bancroft turned to Dawn and handed her two small daggers. She stood holding them limp in her hands, confused and uncomfortable. She had never held a weapon before. Bancroft noticed the hesitation in Dawn's eyes. He brought his hands to hers and closed her fingers around the bone handles of the daggers.

"Better safe than sorry." He waited until Dawn's gaze met his. "Just do me a favor and keep them on your person." He let go of her hands, then placed his hands on Joey and smiled. Dawn watched as Bancroft closed his eyes and kissed Josiah on the forehead, she could feel the love and affection he carried for Josiah. When Bancroft looked back into her eyes, she noticed something more: fear.

Bancroft stepped closer to Ulrica and embraced her tightly. For the first time, Dawn noticed how much taller Ulrica was than her husband. Bancroft reached up to touch her tanned cheek, and she smiled and lowered her head to his.

"It's been awhile, huh love?" Bancroft whispered. Ulrica nodded her head and held his hand firmly to her cheek. "I love you, Ulrica," Bancroft said out loud before passionately kissing his wife.

After one more embrace, Ulrica went to open the door. She turned around with her hand still on her handle. She looked around, making sure she hadn't forgotten anything, tapped her hand on her bag, and pushed the door open. They all solemnly exited the cabin. Dawn stood awkwardly in the sun. It seemed like an eternity had passed since she had seen it. *Has it really only been one day?* she thought.

Bancroft stepped in front of her, taking his place as the leader of the group, searching the forest in front of them. Dawn's grip tightened on her daggers; she began to grow anxious about what lie before them. She had forgotten to ask where they were going or how long they would be underway. She had put all her faith in Ulrica and Bancroft, who, as of yesterday, were strangers to her. She quickly looked down at Josiah, who looked back at her seemingly wide awake and completely unafraid. Dawn found comfort in Josiah's tranquility, smiled, and mouthed "I love you" before turning to watch Ulrica close the door.

Ulrica let out a deep sigh as she locked the wooden door of

the cabin. Her beautiful face was marred with pain, and a tiny silver bead fell from eyes. Ulrica joined the others, and with a heavy heart, she took her husband's hand and did not look back.

Chapter 5

Retreat

Bancroft took the first step and the women followed. They didn't travel the beaten path; they crossed it and went directly into the foliage of the forest. As they scaled trees and made their way through the wilderness, Dawn began having flashbacks of her failed attempt to outrun Tucker. Everything around her looked slightly familiar and wildly new at the same time. Dawn tried desperately to fight off the memories of her last moments with her mother's murderer, but despite her efforts, they came to haunt her, one vision after another.

Bancroft kept a watchful eye on their surroundings. He never looked down to watch where he was stepping and miraculously never lost his footing. One hand held his broad ax and the other held the bag close to his side.

Ulrica seemed on edge. Dawn noticed that she looked nervous outside her element. Out here, encased in the darkness of the trees that towered above them like black ghosts, Ulrica was not in control and it showed. Dawn remembered that in the cabin, she seemed to float about lightly, her skirt swaying like the blades of tall grass on a breezy day. Now her movements were wild and erratic, and her head snapped left and right as she walked with a hunched back, as though she were expecting a blow from some unseen enemy.

They walked in silence, huddled together, keeping Dawn and the baby in the middle. Their footsteps were silent, muffled by the soft forest ground. They walked for what seemed like hours. Dawn watched as the thick, dark forest began to thin, allowing more sun to poke through the leaves, revealing a forest that was green and flourishing, littered with oaks, elms, birch, and other deciduous trees Dawn did not recognize. This was Dawn's favorite type of forest. The sweet, damp smells filled her head, reminding her of home. She no longer thought about Tucker or her great-uncle's cabin, and she actually began to enjoy the journey. With the thinning forest also came less debris. Dawn could see further into the forest than ever before, giving her a sense of comfort, which quickly turned to anxiety.

"I'm watching you."

All at once it seemed to get darker. Dawn noticed, and she was sure the others did too. Bancroft tightened his grip on the wooden handle of his broad ax, and Ulrica was so close, Dawn could feel her hot breath on her neck. It seemed as though the forest was becoming some sinister entity that was more and more aware of its intruders with every step they took.

Dawn didn't dare speak, in fear of the Gidlies, in fear of evil, in fear of the unknown and everything else. They were so close to each other now that if Bancroft were to suddenly stop, Dawn would surely pierce his side with her daggers. As the forest grew still darker, Dawn could feel the tension growing. She felt that she could cut the air with her daggers. Every now and then Bancroft would raise his right fist to his shoulder, which would cause the group to stop dead in its tracks. They all held their breath as he cautiously scanned the forest for all the dangers Dawn was afraid of. When no threat was discovered, he would glance back to his group, lower his fist, nod his head, and they would continue their journey.

It seemed to Dawn that a whole day had passed. *The sun must be setting soon,* she thought. She grew weary and was overwhelmed with thoughts and emotions as they walked in silence through the dark forest. *Where are we going? Are we still in danger? Exactly how much danger? Are we there yet?* She felt she could no longer hold in her anxieties. She opened her mouth to speak, but before a word could form on her tongue, Ulrica grabbed her shoulder, whipped her around, and stared Dawn dead in her eyes. Ulrica shook her head slowly from left to right, a look of dire warning burned in her eyes. It became very clear, very fast, that Dawn was to remain silent. She turned back around and the small group kept trekking in silence, deeper into the darkening forest.

Dawn concentrated on her steps and once again fell into the murky pool of contemplation. Pondering the facts, she thought how weird it was that they were still alive, although they were dead. *What will become of me? What will become of Joey?*

When she lifted her head to direct her gaze forward, she noticed little lights popping up all around her. At first she thought they were fireflies, but when she looked closer, she realized they were tiny sparks. Tiny, floating sparks. Out of sheer curiosity, she held out her hand to touch one. As the spark gently bounced off of her palm, she quickly retracted her hand. It burned her shell and left a light-purple mark where it hit. Dawn immediately went to shield Josiah with the scarf. Before she could, she looked into his eyes; they embodied two, blue oceans of water, whose faces reflected the light of the burning embers like bright sparkling fireworks. The lights reminded Dawn of the cabin and the glowing candle in the window, and a feeling of warmth washed over her. She smiled sweetly before finally covering him again. As she raised her head again, she was astonished to see that the group had been engulfed in a spiraling cloud of floating sparks as bright and fire-orange as the sun. The sparks formed an illuminated ball and encircled the four as they walked through the forest.

Once Dawn realized the sparks were not a threat, she took the light-brown scarf off Josiah's face. and He seemed relieved to be able to see again and was immediately mesmerized by the beauty surrounding them. Dawn thought she saw him smile before she was hypnotized once again by the flickering in his wondrous eyes. She smiled. His eyes always gave her a sense of calm, and now that was coupled with a welcomed sense of peace, radiating from the sphere around them.

Everything is going to be all right!, she thought, just before Ulrica violently turned around and grabbed her by the shoulder. Frightened, Dawn watched as Ulrica swiftly covered Josiah's face with the blanket. She stood frozen as she watched the golden sphere of comfort fall like a damaged golden curtain to the ground, taking all its warmth with it. As the sparks cascaded to the floor, they singed a circle around them. There was a hissing sound as though air were being slowly let out of a tire. Within seconds, the sparks dispersed outward from their feet, revealing the blackened forest floor around them.

Without saying a word, Ulrica put her hands over Dawn's and forced her to tighten her grip on her daggers. Dawn watched in fear as Ulrica's hair began to rise, as if there were some static charge above her head. Her grip tightened around Dawn's fragile hands. Dawn wanted to pull back in pain, but she just stood in shock as she witnessed Ulrica transform. Her beautiful, slender hands became hairy claws. Her mouth grew larger, as if someone were pulling Ulrica's head back by her ears. She was beastly.

"Behind," she growled. It seemed like she wanted to say more, but the rest of the sentence was lost in a snarl.

"Get between us, Dawn," whispered Bancroft as he dared a glance back. "And for god's sake, pull up your weapons."

Dawn was now between the two. She had never held a weapon until this day and felt desperately uncomfortable as she awkwardly held her daggers in front of her. Ulrica was swaying left and right with a hunched back, brandishing her tomahawks. She was ready for any attack from behind. Bancroft stood in front of Dawn, still as a statue, listening and holding his broad ax. Dawn could hear his fingers rubbing against the wooden handle until he found his grip. Dawn's body grew rigid; the suspense was deadly. *What the bloody hell is going on here?* she thought.

"I'm watching you."

Dawn clumsily spun around, missing Bancroft's back by centimeters with the sharp tip of her daggers.

"Stay still," Bancroft demanded, "and watch it with those things!"

They didn't hear that? Dawn thought to herself as she looked panicked in every direction.

It was then that Dawn saw him emerge from behind a tree—a slinky, thin man whose yellow hair was tied back in a ponytail that hung over his left shoulder like a golden rope. He wore a black button-up shirt, black skinny jeans, and black biker boots. He had black leather straps that crossed his chest, no doubt keeping the two curved swords he was carrying in place. He was clean and his clothes looked pressed. His demeanor was perfect yet treacherous, as though he were making a statement, standing there in the middle of the thick, dark forest without one hair out of place.

"My birdies told me you'd be coming this way." He had a British accent and his voice was deep, not at all fitting for his slender frame. "So, I thought we'd make a party."

Bancroft took a defensive step back, "Well, then, you should have brought more to the party," he scoffed. Bancroft's voice was deep and smoky, but nowhere near as deep as the stranger's.

The stranger lowered his head and dramatically crossed his arms as he reached for the long wooden handles behind his shoulders. With ease, he pulled out two slender curved katanas and lowered them to his sides. He raised his head and smiled as he held his stance.

"Who says I'm alone?" the stranger grinned, showing his crooked teeth as a black angry bear came from behind the brush on all fours. The bear's hair was dreadlocked and dirty. Thick, long locks swayed from side to side with each slow step he took. When he reached the stranger's side he stopped, raised his huge black head, and revealed his yellow eyes. Two monstrous fangs jutted upward from his jaw, dripping heavily with saliva. The bear turned his massive head toward his partner and snarled, sending his saliva flying in all directions.

The stranger in black chuckled arrogantly at the sight of his companion. "Hello, mate. Thanks for coming! Good googly moogly, you're a big one!" He laughed and gave the bear a friendly push with his skinny body. The bear playfully pushed back before stretching his back, extending his large hindquarters into the air. Dawn watched in fear as his heavy front paws reached out. His long black claws cut into the damp forest floor, churning the rich, dark earth as he pulled his body back together. She gasped as the beast rose onto his hind legs.

"GRRRRROOOOOOOOAAU!" His growl was deafening. Dawn's body shuddered and she instinctively backed up. She slid awkwardly on the burned moss below her feet. The bear hunched his broad shoulders and let his thick forearms hang loose as he eyed his prey. "GRROOOOOOOOOOAU!" he roared again as his hungry eyes rested on the bundle in Dawn's arms.

"Damn Gidly," Bancroft whispered. If Bancroft was afraid, he did not show it. Ulrica now faced forward; her chest heaved as she growled and snarled to herself between breaths. Dawn glanced at her and was suddenly comforted to have this beastly woman standing next to her.

"You *cannot* pass." The pale stranger took one of his blades and made a line on the forest floor. "Turn back now and we might spare your lives," the slender man commanded.

"You bastard!" Bancroft spat on the forest floor. "Do you think I am going to turn my back on you?"

"As you wish." The grizzly Gidly began to slowly advance in the direction of the baby. Dawn closed her eyes and raised her head. Her lips moved as she silently whispered a prayer. When she opened her eyes, she saw the bright-orange sparks flicker above them in the treetops. She blinked a few times in fear that she was hallucinating.

It was then the sparks came back in a fierce burning cloud, forming a fiery tornado in the middle of the sparing group. Loose leaves and twigs caught fire and were sucked into the spiraling funnel of flames. Dawn watched in awe as the column grew hotter and brighter. She was instantly reminded of the book of Exodus in the Bible. She remembered how God saved Moses and his people from the Egyptians by sending a burning pillar of cloud. With an ear-popping **SNAP** and in the blink of an eye, the sparks imploded in a blinding flash of hot-white energy, and the ashes of the forest floor came raining down on all of them. In the middle where the fire once raged, standing a statuesque eight feet tall, was a magnificent bird. His neck was long like a peacock; his oval-shaped body was planted firm on his long ostrich-like legs. His beak and talons looked as though they were made of pure gold, and his feathers were the color of embers burning in a fire. His bright-orange tail feathers were gracefully long; they resembled the train of a luxurious wedding gown as they rested at his side. His entire posture demanded reverence and ignited envy.

"A phoenix," Dawn whispered in disbelief. The sudden presence of a phoenix seemed to surprise no one but her. She glanced up to the heavens that were hidden behind the treetops and smiled, thankful. It was undoubtedly a gift from God.

The phoenix positioned himself at the head of the group. Bancroft stood ready for action on his left with Dawn, Ulrica, and the baby on his right.

"CAW!" the phoenix screeched and snapped his golden beak at the black dreaded beast. "CAAAAAAW!" the phoenix screeched again, and with a flap, opened his wings, revealing a yellow undercoat that singed the eyes. Dawn stood behind the phoenix, mesmerized by his entire existence. The colors of his wings were remarkably bright and vivid. She had the urge to reach out and touch them, just to see if they would burn her.

"GRRRAOU!" The Gidly roared and reared onto his hind legs, then snarled and clawed at the forest floor in front of him. The phoenix kept his magnificent wings extended as his golden chest swelled. He snapped ferociously with his beak, warning his challenger not to come any closer. Dawn watched as the two began to dance: beauty and the beast. She felt Ulrica's heavy claws on her shoulder, pulling her backward and toward Bancroft. Dawn allowed herself to be moved like a chess piece and continued to watch the fight. Once the bear noticed that the distance between him and his prey had grown, he went into a fury. He roared and lunged himself into the fire-orange body of the phoenix. The phoenix cawed as he pushed the bear off of him with his golden talons. The bear regained his balance and lunged his massive black body toward the bird again, this time in full force. The phoenix was ready for his attack and caught the bear by his scruffy black neck in one of his golden talons. With one fluid movement, he flapped his wings and carried the bear high into the canopy of the forest. There in the air the two beasts continued to dance. The phoenix squawked angrily as the bear swung an open paw at his chest, blindly hitting the mark. The two entangled creatures dropped clumsy, crashing into the branches above their companions. The man in black and Bancroft had no problem dodging the debris that carelessly rained down.

"Dawn!" Bancroft yelled before Ulrica tackled her, being careful not to harm the baby. A couple of rogue twigs landed around them, and the main branch crashed heavily onto the ground, missing them by inches.

"Thank you," Dawn whispered to Ulrica's beastly face. Even through the wild hair and the transformed face, Dawn could see Ulrica's disapproving eyes. Dawn tried to get up, but Ulrica pushed her back down to the ground.

"Stay," Ulrica growled and then snarled at Dawn. Dawn obeyed and sat on the forest floor, straddled by Ulrica's hairy legs. Dawn was immediately thankful that Ulrica wore a long skirt and that the skirt remained in place during her transformation.

All heads were facing upward, watching the intense battle. The phoenix was able to grab one of the bear's shoulders with his free talon. With the other talon still secure around the raging beast's thick neck, he squeezed and twisted. An agonizing sound came from the Gidly, and he went limp in the talons of the phoenix.

"CAW!" the phoenix screeched after his victory before opening his golden talons, allowing his enemy to plummet to the forest floor.

The skinny man frowned as he watched his companion smash lifeless onto the ground. He clinched his jaw, brought his brown eyes up to meet Bancroft's steel-blue gaze, and raised his katanas. Without speaking a word, he charged at Bancroft with alarming speed. Holding both katanas high in the air behind him, he looked almost birdlike himself.

"Speedster," Bancroft whispered but didn't move. Ulrica crouched lower, now almost sitting on Dawn, who was happy to be trapped between Ulrica's legs on the soft undergrowth of the forest. Dawn lay on her side, propped up by her elbow, and tightly cradled Josiah as she shielded him, holding the dagger in front of her. She kept her eyes on the fight, desperately trying not to blink. Ulrica seemed to have the same strategy. Her eyes were wide as she watched the stranger dash to her husband.

The two men were so different in size and shape and style that Dawn had a hard time guessing what the outcome would be. Both women waited silently as the speedster began to clash with Bancroft. Time seemed suspended, and in an instant, it was obvious who the victor would be.

Dawn watched as Bancroft jumped into the air, dodging the slice of the swords. He landed firmly behind his attacker, who was still crouched from a failed attack and visibly surprised that he had missed his small, bulky target. In a split second, Bancroft spun with his broad ax firmly planted in both hands. Another agonizing yell broke the silence of the forest as the stranger fell defeated onto his face. His soul began to seep into the air—metallic blue from his side where Bancroft's ax still jutted from his ribs. With a kick of his worn tan boots, Bancroft turned the man on his back.

"Surrender and we will heal you." Bancroft was now on his

knee, bracing himself with the handle on his broad ax. He looked more like a priest giving a last prayer over the mortally injured man than a warrior who had just slain his enemy.

"There is no saving my soul. I have failed her." The stranger looked Bancroft in his eyes as he reached a weary hand to touch his knee. "And in truth, kind soul, I would never have given you this option." He turned his gaze to the forest canopy and watched as his soul floated like a blue string attached to the end of an invisible balloon. As he admired his soul he whispered, "Please, finish me off." With those last words, Bancroft stood above his golden-haired opponent, grabbed the wooden handle of his ax, and brought the iron blade down with a swift crushing sound. There was no sound from the stranger this time. He peacefully closed his eyes as his glowing soul flowed up and out of his body, dispersing metallic-blue effervescence into the air.

Bancroft stood and bowed his head in silence as he pulled his ax from the stranger's shell. He turned to look at the women. Ulrica was no longer squatting over Dawn; she had risen and was slowly regaining her form. Her hair fell down like silk onto her shoulders. She groaned and growled as her claws fell off one by one onto the forest floor, revealing her beautiful, healthy nails and smooth hands.

Bancroft looked away to Dawn. He hated to see his wife transform. He knew how painful the whole process was and he couldn't bear to see his wife in pain, but more than that, he hated to see his wife in her animal form. It gave him nightmares and reminded him that she didn't need him to take care of her. Every time Ulrica transformed, Bancroft was reminded of the people he left behind, the people who did depend on him, who did need him, and the memories pained him so. He walked over to Dawn, who was still on the forest floor by Ulrica's legs, clutching Josiah in one arm and her dagger in the other. Bancroft reached out a thick hand to help her up, but Dawn didn't notice him. She was still looking at the speedster, watching the last of his beautiful soul disperse into the air.

She looked terribly lost and horrified.

The phoenix came back down with astonishing silence. His presence seemed to awaken Dawn. She looked just in time to see him land gracefully, his divine fire-orange wings covering much of the soft, burnt ground. His long, lovely tail swished as it landed curled at the side of his body.

"Dawn," Bancroft gently motioned with his open hand. Dawn thankfully reached up and then hesitated when she noticed he still had a smear of blue on his hand. He quickly wiped the back of his hand on his jeans and examined it before once again offering it to her. Bancroft smiled awkwardly, not at all sure what to say. Dawn smiled back and took his hand. "Are you okay?" Bancroft whispered as she let him pull her up. Bancroft smiled at Dawn, it was in this moment he realized, here was someone he could help, someone who needed him. When he was sure she could stand firmly on both feet and wouldn't topple over, he snuck a look under the blanket.

Dawn looked at the phoenix and watched as Ulrica went to greet him. Her legs were still transforming with each step she took. By the time she reached the giant fire bird, she was her exceptionally alluring self. Dawn looked at the two, vaguely aware of the silly sounds Bancroft was making to Josiah. Never in her life had she seen a more exquisite sight than the one that was before her.

Bancroft brought his head back out from under the blanket and uncovered Josiah's face in the process. For the first time, everyone was smiling. Bancroft looked into Dawn's eyes. She held his gaze and was slightly taken aback as she witnessed a silver tear run down his round face. He reached up his hand and pulled her head down to his by the scruff of her neck. He gently kissed her forehead, and then with more compassion, he kissed Josiah.

The two walked over to the others. Ulrica was mending some of the smaller wounds of the phoenix with a pale-green putty. She rubbed the putty into the wound that bled gold. He ruffled his feathers, looking more like a little bird bathing in puddle than the fierce beast he was. He took a step back with his golden talons as Bancroft pushed Dawn toward him. Standing only a foot from his grand golden beak, Dawn noticed the bird's luminous emerald eyes. The bird cooed gently as he nudged his beak toward the baby. Dawn uncovered Josiah's face once again, and the bird cocked his head to the side and let out a tender tweet.

He then took two steps back, spread his fiery wings, and bowed. He took off with immense force, blowing their hair back and spiraling underneath the canopy before gracefully crashing through the forest ceiling, causing branches and twigs to come crashing down. The sun flooded through the hole he made, and for the first time in what seemed like forever, Dawn felt the warm, golden rays of the sun kiss her skin. There the three stood in the single ray of light.

"Beautiful," Dawn whispered.

"Show off," grumbled Bancroft through a grin.

Chapter 6

Welcome Home

*T*he four travelers found themselves on the brink of a small village, surrounded by the dark forest they had just fled from. The village sat peacefully in a ring of towering maple and elm trees. The sun glistened off of their leaves and onto a circle of cabins, leaving the grass below flooded in its brilliance. The thick green blades shimmered as though they were made of glass. The ocean of green and gold left Dawn breathless. She had an overwhelming urge to paint, even though she had never held a paintbrush in her life.

Ulrica brushed her hand along Dawn's back to keep her moving. Their footsteps became silent as they left the acorn-littered forest bed and entered the clearing. A soft breeze brushed past them, rustling the trees and blowing the stray hairs that framed Ulrica's face. She turned to look at Dawn and flashed a smile so bright it rivaled the sun. Bancroft put his hand on Josiah's head and kissed him gently as they walked closer to the halo of cabins.

As they approached the cabins, Dawn noticed they were very much like the one they left behind that morning, only these were sturdier and well kept. Some had small gardens flowering with herbs; others were adorned with honeysuckle and lavender. Despite the individuality among the humble homes, the design was the same; each had one small wooden door coupled with one small square window on its right. In the center of the circle of cabins was a stone well, its walls made of smooth gray stones and thick green moss. There was no bucket and no rope. As Dawn looked about her, she wondered what the well was for. She had no memory of drinking or eating since she entered the realm.

Why the garden? Why the well? she thought to herself as the four slowly made their way closer to the center of the village. Before she could ponder the thought any longer, Ulrica tightly seized Dawn by the elbow and began quickly leading her toward one of the cabins on the opposite side of the circle. She felt a large hand on her back and turned to see that two large black men, both wielding long swords, had come to usher them in. Two more men emerged seemingly from the inside of the well. They too were brandishing weapons, weapons Dawn had never seen before. These strangers formed a tight belt, keeping Dawn in the middle. Not one greeting was exchanged. No one looked happy to see them. In fact, no one paid Dawn any attention at all; they all looked about—some in the air and some into the forest. It was then that Dawn realized these villagers were watching for something or someone ominous. The immense feeling of security and warmth the sun provided only a few minutes ago was replaced with a searing heat that seemed to single them out, placing them firmly on the radar. There were no longer any shadows in which to hide.

"I'm watching you." Dawn swung her head around in panic to see where the mysterious voice was coming from. Bancroft noticed her sudden spike in insecurity. He looked into Dawn's worried eyes, but before she could begin to try and explain what was happening to her, they were escorted into a cabin.

From the outside, the cabin was bare with no decorations, no garden. A singular flame flickered with a warm familiarity in the window. Once inside, Dawn was placed in a chair that sat between the door and the window. As Dawn waited for everyone to enter the cabin, she sat longing to hear their boots shuffle on the aged wooden planks that made up the floor. She had hoped, now that they were among friends, that some normalcy would enter their lives. For a fleeting moment, she had envisioned a small room full of happy people. They were all drinking tea and playing catch-up.

The wooden door to the cabin slammed shut and clinked as Ulrica promptly locked it. Dawn stood to look out of the window. The cabin was quiet, so unlike her mind, which was full of questions that were rattling fiercely against the sides of her brain. *Who are these people?* she thought as she watched her escorts scurry through the courtyard and back to their respective cabins. *Are they bodyguards?* she questioned herself silently as she stood there, instinctively rocking the still-bundled Josiah in her arms. *What are they guarding me from? Am I a prisoner?* Ulrica leaned in front of her as though Dawn were not even there, standing alone in front of the small square window. The corners of her mouth turned and formed a sneaky grin before she gently blew out the candle that sat on the windowsill. Dawn watched in astonishment as the world outside began to dissolve. She watched as all the colors faded—first the crisp green of trees and then the earthy browns that gave the cabins their warm character. The thick, rich, green grass faded last. It was as though someone were erasing the entire village, slowly and thoroughly, until all that was left behind was a blank canvas. Dawn stood motionless for a few more seconds, wondering who exactly was performing the disappearing act. Was it the outside world that vanished or was she the one who no longer existed? She turned around dumbfounded and sat back down on the hard wooden chair. She looked down at the bundle in her arms and uncovered Josiah's face. She leaned down and kissed him on his wide, soft forehead and felt hopeless, wanting nothing more than to lose herself in his big eyes.

"Where am I?" she whispered in a daze. No one answered. As Dawn looked up, she realized the layout of this cabin was the same as the one they left behind. A candle was aglow in the center of the room on a large, dark, smooth wooden table. The counter in the back was bigger, and its granite top seemed to shine in the candlelight. Three large wooden chairs with light-green cushions were tucked underneath it. Bancroft was bracing himself on the fourth chair as he pulled his boots and socks off. After wiggling his bare toes and scratching the sole of one foot, he stuck his grey wool socks into his boots before placing them underneath the table and taking a seat. Once he was properly seated, he took out his short cherry wood pipe and began loading it.

Ulrica was already in her element, behind the stone-top counter. She had emptied the contents of her satchel. It appeared as though everything had its place up there. She never hesitated. Ulrica seemed so at ease with her movements and so comfortable in her shell that in this moment, Dawn envied her. Dawn longed for a place in the room; she longed for a reason to exist. From the chair under the window, everything looked as though it were back to normal. Everyone was at home, and Dawn had never felt so alone.

"Are we under attack?" Dawn spoke softly. Ulrica glanced up from her work; her eyes sent Dawn a message that she didn't understand.

"This was a dangerous journey." Ulrica began speaking, but not directly to Dawn. "Had it not been for Griffen, we might not have made it."

"Where are the other houses?" Dawn questioned louder. "How long have I been dead? How many people actually live here? And why the well? I haven't drunken or eaten anything since I have been here. Why is that?" With each question, Dawn's voice grew louder. No one answered her questions; they just pretended not to hear her. For a dreadful moment, Dawn feared that she too had vanished along with the world outside the window.

Ulrica looked toward Dawn and gave her the same look as before. Her dark soulful eyes were trying to communicate with Dawn's bright inquisitive ones, but they weren't speaking the same language. Dawn furrowed her brow, trying to understand. Ulrica looked away before making her way from behind the counter. Dawn sighed in relief. *Maybe she's coming to tell me* she thought. An naive smile began to spread across Dawn's face. But instead of coming over to console Dawn, Ulrica stopped at the wooden door next to the small window, jiggled her hand in her apron pocket, and blew white powder at the door.

"I almost forgot!" Ulrica said loudly, smiling at Bancroft, who half-heartedly returned her smile and shrugged off the mishap.

"And what *is* it with the white powder?" Dawn was frustrated and flirting with hysteria and was not willing to give up. After a journey in silence they were finally allowed to speak, and no one was speaking to her. Bancroft leaned back in his chair and stretched his bare feet out in front of him, puffing heavily on his pipe.

Infuriated, Dawn looked down on the bundle in her arms and found a tiny bit of courage. She had a right to know these things. Dawn stood up and screamed, "WHY AREN'T YOU ANSWERING ME? DID I DO SOMETHING WRONG?" She took the few steps to the table and looked down at Bancroft who was now attempting to blow smoke rings and failing miserably. Frustrated and defeated, she took the seat across from him. She hunched over Josiah and stared into the flame of the candle that stood in the middle of the table. As she lost herself in the flicker of orange, yellow, and blue, she remembered the bird. "What was that back there that traveled with us? Was that a phoenix?" This time she looked up at Ulrica, who, to her astonishment, was watching her with still hands and worried eyes.

"Yes," Ulrica whispered. "That was our dear friend, Griffen." Ulrica gripped the edges of the counter and leaned forward, gazing at Dawn with the same heavy look and biting her lower lip. Dawn perked up in her seat. She still wasn't sure what the gaze meant or why no one answered any of the other questions, but she was relieved that she at least got to talk about this.

"Griffen?" stated Dawn with a perplexed look on her face. "I thought griffins were the flying lion creatures."

"There's a lot you don't know, princess." A cold voice cut through the warm ambience of the room. "For example, Griffen just risked his very existence . . ." said a thin, pale man with a long, straight nose who stepped out of the shadows in the back of the room, ". . . and ours to bring *you* here to safety."

"Good afternoon, Jorge," Bancroft sneered, as the stranger in black walked up to the table. Bancroft pulled in his bare feet as the apparently unwelcome stranger took a seat at the table between Dawn and himself.

"He broke the treaty, Bancroft. He's not allowed this far back. You know that!" Jorge had crisp, black, calculating eyes that sunk into his narrow, sharp face; they were currently set on Dawn. His fine lips curled at her as though he were looking at a pile of dung and not a beautiful young woman. She was trivial and insignificant, and he made sure she felt that. Dawn lowered her head to her body as if by habit, trying to escape his disdain. "You should have told him to go."

"Are you out of your mind?" Bancroft slammed his pipe on the table, spilling its charred insides on the smooth wooden surface. His angry head began to glow pink. "He wouldn't have given us cover if we didn't *need* him!"

"He was guiding and protecting us. We would have never made it without him," Ulrica chimed in. Unlike her quick-tempered husband, her composure never faltered and her words showed no emotion, as if the events of the day had no effect on her.

Dawn watched as Jorge shifted his weight in his chair so he faced Bancroft, successfully giving her the cold shoulder. She shuddered and held Josiah closer to her bosom.

"We have been living here in peace for quite some time. Fighting battles we *knew* we could win." Jorge looked over his shoulder as though he could feel Dawn watching. She quickly lowered her head again, suddenly eerily aware of the weapon she still held in her hand. Jorge looked at Ulrica, who was shaking her head in disappointment as she bagged some green paste. He smirked, satisfied with Ulrica's disapproval of Dawn's submission, and turned back to Bancroft. "With the treaty broken, we will be getting visitors we cannot handle."

"The Gidlies came to our house first!" Bancroft shouted. "What were we to do?" Bancroft's fists were clenched and he sat on the edge of his chair, thrusting his round head forward. Ulrica said nothing. She stood behind her counter, staring coldly at Jorge, while her hands remained busy crushing leaves. Dawn slowly raised her head again, her face a fusion of anger, hate, fear, and compassion. When she looked at Bancroft, his defiance, his inability to stand down, his actions, filled her heart with strength. This sensation was unfamiliar to her. The warmth spread outward from her chest; she slowly raised her chin and straightened her back.

"All this trouble for some silly girl. You all are so selfish," said Jorge. Dawn let the warmth turn to fire inside of her. The hairs on her neck began to rise and the grip on her dagger tightened "We all have missions here, we all have a purpose." He looked around the room as though he had a huge audience. "And you just disrupted it all." Jorge turned his skinny body so he could look at Dawn, who was trying with all her might to be brave. "You should have let them have the girl and been done with it!"

"WHY YOU POMPOUS JACKASS!" Bancroft stood with such force that his wooden chair went thumping to the floor. Jorge sat back and crossed his arms.

Although Bancroft was standing, he was not much taller than Jorge, who had silver beads of sweat forming on his brow. Dawn watched intently. Never had anyone stood up for her like this. She felt important and strong. She placed her dagger on the table and sat back in her chair. She switched Josiah from one arm to the other and let a smile crack her lips; she thoroughly enjoyed watching Jorge sweat. She really liked not being afraid; she really liked having an ally who was willing to throw chairs and get loud. She watched as Bancroft edged closer to Jorge. She felt that even though Bancroft was a foot shorter, he could have easily taken the cold, thin man. She remembered his acrobatics from before and was immensely comforted to have Bancroft on her side.

"That's enough!" bellowed a deep, strong voice from the back of the room, which shook the cabin's very foundation.

Alarmed, Dawn straightened and reached for her dagger as she squinted to the back of the room.

"Well, it's about time. What took you so long, Marlon?" Ulrica smiled. Dawn wondered briefly if anything ever surprised that woman.

"Must you two *always* get at each other's throats?" A man of immense stature emerged from the shadows. His black T-shirt was tight on his body, and his muscles were easily visible through the fabric. He was wearing loose black-and-yellow track pants and black sneakers. He was the complete opposite of the last man who appeared out of the shadows; this giant had a warm glow to his skin and a very handsome face. Dawn noticed one similarity: his eyes looked just as callous and as calculating as Jorge's. "Jorge, we all knew that eventually the day would come when we would no longer have the duty of sitting around picking off the little vermin that try to make their way past us." The giant came closer to Dawn. Strangely, she was not afraid. "We all knew the day would come when we would get the *privilege* to fight, to go to war. That's what we all came down here for, isn't it?"

"That's right, Green Bean," Bancroft shot out. Jorge, obviously hating the name he had just been called, stood up from his chair. His thin body towered over Bancroft like a pine tree would a bush. Bancroft was unaffected by his actions and warned, "Not one more ill word or I swear to you, I will put a hurt on you."

Jorge stepped back and glared at Bancroft. He clearly had more to say, but after weighing his options, he looked at the faces around him and wisely changed his tone.

"Well, what was it that the Gidlies wanted? Surely they didn't break the rules for some little *girl*." Jorge's lip curled like he had taken a sip of curdled milk. Evidently he felt if he could not voice his displeasure, he would show it.

Dawn held his dark gaze this time. She didn't move, she didn't speak, but she refused to look down. She locked her eyes on her attacker with a fierce intensity she didn't know she had. When Jorge looked away from her, she redirected her gaze to Ulrica, who winked at her from behind the counter. Dawn smiled to herself and sat a few centimeters taller for the rest of the day.

"Marlon," Ulrica said, directing her attention to the giant, "we must speak with you." She turned to look into Jorge's pale face. "Alone." Jorge gave the group one last look of detestation and stormed off to the back of the cabin.

Ulrica, unimpressed by Jorge's behavior, came from behind the island and tossed a tweed sack to Marlon. He opened the sack and poured a light-blue dust into his huge hand. He filled his lungs with air and blew into the middle of the room. His breath was so mighty that the shimmering dust filled the entire room and hung in the air, suspended, unaffected by the rules of gravity. Dawn smiled as she looked about her. She moved her hand up to touch the dust, leaving an open trail where her hand had traveled. Her eyes grew wide with astonishment as she watched the sparkling dust fill the space. She got up and walked to the window, leaving a clear path behind her. She watched as that space filled itself as well. She tried to look out of the window again and realized she couldn't see anything outside the range of the dust. Like an inverted bubble, she could clearly see everything within the dust cloud. She took a seat in the wooden chair below the window, numb with astonishment.

"Did you lock that door, Marlon? I don't want him sneaking in and coming into our bubble."

"Don't worry, Ulrica. I locked it." The giant grinned and shrugged his massive shoulders. "I think we would notice him trying to sneak into the cloud anyway, don't you?"

"Yes, but I would rather him, well, anyone, not know of our use of this cloud." Ulrica carefully added, "I don't want suspicions to rise or doubt to be cast."

Marlon nodded in agreement. Dawn looked at the three standing in a circle in the middle of the blue dust; she looked on like an injured player watching from the sidelines, and that's how she felt—like
she didn't belong, as though the game weren't meant for her. She sat
on the chair below the window listening, rocking Josiah, wondering
if she even still existed. She had trekked all this way and still none of
her questions were answered. Quite the opposite. More were raised.

"So, are the rumors true?" Marlon's voice boomed. He squinted
his face and braced himself as though the sky were going to fall.
"Sorry," he whispered.

"Not so loud, big guy!" Bancroft chuckled heartily. "You'll
puncture the cloud. Trust me, you don't want any of this to leak out
until you're ready for it!" With that he patted the giant on his back
with confidence and took a seat at the table next to his wife, the blue
cloud filling his wake.

"Yes," Ulrica spoke, sitting with perfect posture on her chair.
"Yes, I'm afraid they are."

Marlon inhaled deeply as he turned to Dawn. "May I see him?"

Dawn was caught off guard, surprised to have been called on.
Her hands trembled as she uncovered Josiah's face. The giant came
closer and bent down on one knee. He covered his mouth with his
enormous hand and gasped the way grandparents do after seeing
their grandchildren for the first time. Marlon directed his coal-black
eyes to Ulrica and spoke from behind his hand as if he were shielding
the baby.

"Are you sure this is the child?"

"Why else would the Gidlies have come?" Bancroft answered,
speaking through his teeth to keep his freshly lit pipe from falling.
The smoke from his pipe made pink trails through the light-blue
cloud, like the swirls in a Van Gogh painting.

"They too could have been mistaken, could they not?" Marlon whispered, staring at the baby. His hand was no longer over

his mouth but was instead reaching for Dawn, who was watching the smoke rise, smiling as it mixed and swirled, forming lavender clouds. She was startled when she felt the touch of another push her hair to the side. She was slightly nervous when she learned it was the touch of the giant, but pleasantly surprised to feel how gentle his touch was.

"Please," he lowered his hand, "I beseech you, tell me your story."

Dawn glanced at Bancroft and Ulrica, and after finding approval in their eyes began telling her story. She started at the beginning. She spoke of the beatings, the stillbirth, the cat finding the baby. She spoke of the lies she told to everyone, to the immediate and constant joy Josiah brought to her life, until their horrific end. She sat and relived her story as she remembered it from the night before, smiling at the highs and crying at the lows. The giant sat still on the floor before her and soaked up every word. Ulrica and Bancroft did not move. It was also their first time hearing Dawn's story in its entirety.

When her memories ran out, Dawn closed with, "And that's all. I found the cabin and that's all." She closed her lips and slightly bowed her head before jerking it back up and adding, "Could someone please answer my questions now?"

To her dismay, as she looked around, she saw that the cloud had dispersed and nighttime had fallen. Marlon was already standing, patting his pants down, and Ulrica and Bancroft were pushing their wooden chairs under the table. She knew no one would answer her questions. Depressed, she looked down at Josiah and sighed.

Jorge did not go far after Ulrica's dismissal. He left the room and heard the key turn as the door was locked behind him. Instead of following the stairs down into the basement, he turned and pressed his ear to the wooden door. Silence. He heard nothing. He snuffed at the door and ran into the basement. He made his way down the corridor of earthen walls and past many doors to the left and right until he finally stopped at a door that looked just like all the others. He tapped a sequence of knocks and the door creaked open. Jorge entered the room, dark with no windows.

"They are planning something." He closed the door and took a seat at a round wooden table that was in the middle of the room. He felt a hand on his shoulder and looked up to see a woman's beautiful round face staring back at him. She gently smiled as she sat in the chair next to him. He reached out and squeezed her hand and returned her smile with his own charming grin. He let her hand go and redirected his attention to the two large black men who were sitting across from him. Everyone watched him, hanging on to his next words. "I think the rumors are true."

The woman gasped, and the two men hit the table in unison with closed fists. "Was the baby there?" the female asked, reaching out her left hand to touch Jorge's skinny forearm.

"Yes," Jorge said, looking first to the others and then focusing on her brown eyes. He resisted the urge to reach up and caress her plump rosy cheeks. Maribelle made him forget, and that was one of the reasons he loved her. He had to force himself to keep his mind on the topic at hand. He broke her gaze and focused on the twins. "You know, a phoenix brought them."

The twins shook their heads in unison. They were strong men, with skin so dark they looked like they had been dipped in ink.

"We were there to escort them in," Benjamin, the brother on the left, said in a deep voice. He was sitting with his back straight, his overalls tight against his bulging chest. "Are we sure this is the right baby?"

"Well, it fits the timetable," Samuel, his twin, replied. He was slouched in his chair with his arms, which resembled black cannons, across his chest. "If this is the chosen child, then he would be the right age. Besides," he added, "how often do we see children or even babies in this realm?"

"We rarely do." Jorge shifted his weight in the chair. "I can't even remember the last time I saw a child." He shook his head as he lied. He could remember. In fact, he saw him every night in his dreams.

"The chosen child," Maribelle repeated silently. "What now?"

"We need more answers," Jorge replied coolly. "I will have a talk with the mother."

"We will meet here again when the appropriate signs are drawn," Benjamin concluded.

Everyone threw up a sign with his or her left hand, signaling the end of the meeting. The two brothers remained at the table and conversed as though they were never part of the prior discussion. Maribelle took Jorge's hand in hers and together they walked toward the door. This time it was Maribelle who took her little round fist and rapped the sequence on the door. Jorge then reached for the handle and opened the door for his woman. Maribelle, although short and stout, left the room with such grace it almost seemed as though she were dancing ballet. Jorge hunkered out after her, closing the door behind them. Once in the seemingly endless underground hallway, Jorge took Maribelle's hand, kissed it lightly, and together they began walking further into the earth.

Chapter 7

The Haven

The first night in her new room was sleepless. Very much like her last room, there was a bed and a night table and one candle that seemed to easily light the entire room and all its earthy corners. Unlike the other room, Dawn was relieved to see that the walls and ceiling were free from roots. She was still very aware that she was underground, but it was comforting not to be reminded by the skinny, twisting toes of the trees and plants above her.

Dawn sat down in the middle of the bed and laid Josiah in between the pillows at the top. She unwrapped him for the first time that day and watched as he stretched his little limbs. He grinned and sighed, visually relieved to be free.

"Eeeee-bababa," Josiah told Dawn as he grabbed blindly with his pudgy fingers, searching for the other limbs he knew were there. "Ma, babababa." Dawn smiled as she watched him squirm to find his feet.

"I know, I know," she replied sympathetically. Josiah smiled at her before finally catching his right foot. His eyes crossed as he pulled his foot closer to examine it. Dawn couldn't tell if he was confused or relieved, but laughed out loud when he promptly stuck his big toe in his mouth.

"Ewwwwwww," Dawn laughed again as her face scrunched together, forming little disapproving wrinkles around her nose. She looked about the empty room for something else for him to chew on. "I need to find you some toys." She bent over and took off her shoes, tucking the white laces neatly into the shoes before placing them squarely at the foot of the bed next to her satchel. She sat on the side of the bed and stretched her legs out into the empty room in front of her. She arched her feet and let out a long sigh as she stretched her arms above her head. After stretching, she combed her long, wavy hair with her fingers and stared blankly at the wall in front of her. She smiled in satisfaction after she managed to run her fingers through without them snagging.

She turned around and propped a pillow against the dirt wall and took her place in the bed, lying on her side next to Josiah. After finally becoming settled in and comfortable, Dawn smiled and looked down at Josiah, who was still devouring his big toe with immense satisfaction. Her smile faded into a frown and worry lines formed on her forehead as her eyebrows pulled together. Josiah looked up to meet Dawn's loving gaze and instead saw the distress on her face. He paused, making a sucking sound as he removed his big baby foot from his mouth and mimicked her expression.

Dawn became heavy with worry. "Where *are* we?" she whispered before feigning a smile. Josiah reached a shiny silver-blue hand up for her to kiss and laughed as she crinkled her nose and pulled away. "Ewwwww!"

"Eeek!" he shrieked happily, as an unnerved Dawn wiped his hand clean with his brown blanket. With one fluid motion, she reached over and grabbed her baby, placing him on her chest as she rolled onto her back. He held his bobble head up and looked into her scared eyes. With one final attempt to make her smile, his whole body wiggled as he laughed and gurgled. He crossed his eyes and blew shiny blue bubbles with his spit before putting his head back down on her chest.

"It's obvious the blue spit doesn't bother you," Dawn giggled. After hearing her happy sounds, Josiah closed his eyes and let his arms rest on her sides. Dawn held Josiah tight to her chest. She loved the way his body rose and fell with their simultaneous breathing. She closed her eyes and tried to imagine that she was in her old home, upstairs in her own room, that the walls just happened to be painted brown. She tried to envision her bed with the white ruffles on the bottom, the fluffy flower-print pillows on the top, and the mattress that seemed to form around her body because it knew her mold. She tried so desperately to wish herself back into her life that when she opened her eyes, she realized that she had stopped breathing, that her chest wasn't moving, and that her eyes were wet and burning from where she had shut them so tightly. She silently wept. It became clear to her that her imagination was nowhere near powerful enough to escape the truths that surrounded her. The sweet aroma of the dark, damp earth was beginning to suffocate her. With Josiah asleep on her chest, she suddenly felt pinned down. Her legs began to prickle with panic. She sat up against the wall, feeling the brown dirt penetrate the fibers on her back. She held Josiah high on her chest as her eyes darted off the walls of her room, which seemed to be coming closer. Josiah squirmed restlessly in her arms; he was beginning to wake.

"Shhhhhh," she whispered into his ear, not wanting to wake him, not wanting him to see her panic. "Shhhhhhh." She placed her face on the top of his head and felt the soft baby curls brush against her skin. She dug her nose into the tuft of his yellow baby hairs and for a moment escaped the putrid smell that encased her. She smiled and breathed his hairs in so deeply they tickled the inside of her nostrils. His scent began to calm her. Her body began to loosen and slide comfortably back onto the pillow. After inhaling deeply once more, the walls returned to their rightful place. She rolled onto her side and held Josiah in the hole her body formed. She kept her nose on his head. The smell of his baby skin offered her peace; she closed her eyes, breathed him in again, and let the scent take her home.

"Mom, why do you think babies smell so good?" Dawn sat on

the floor between her mother's legs holding Josiah.

"I don't know," her mother replied as she brushed her daughter's lustrous locks into a ponytail. "But if I had to guess, I would say it's because they come from God." Dawn shifted on the couch pillow as Josiah stretched. It was awkward only being able to hold him with one arm. Her other arm was still healing in a sling. "That baby smell is there to remind us that they are gifts from God, so precious and innocent."

"Mom," Dawn said smiling, loving the way her mother's hands flowed through her hair as she began braiding a long thick braid down her back, "that's exactly why."

For a moment's time, Dawn forgot she was underground in a stuffy, airless room. For a moment's time, she allowed her memories to take her back home. She remembered the warm summer nights, her mother's full, hearty laugh. Even her cat, Jimmy Bean, came to visit her, tickling her ankles as he purred and wove a pattern between her feet.

If only all her memories were beautiful ones.

"I thought I told yew I wanted pork chops for dinner," Tucker spat as Dawn handed him his dinner in his La-Z-Boy in front of the television.

"I know, but you said chicken first," Dawn began. Tucker grabbed her slender wrist before she could retreat to the kitchen.

"Are you talking back?" Tucker squeezed so hard her knees buckled.

"No, I'm sorry," Dawn said, holding back her cry and trying not to pull away from his bone-crushing grip. "I, I can go make you some pork chops." Tucker's grip loosened. He looked at his plate of fried chicken in his other hand and contemplated for a second. His red eyebrows crooked with thought. He looked again at the full plate and sighed. Dawn dared a breath of relief as she witnessed his brows smooth and his eyes turn to the football game. He finally released her wrist, throwing it to his side.

"Go get me a Coke," he mumbled.

Dawn hurriedly went to the kitchen, cradling her throbbing wrist close to her body. She opened the refrigerator door, grabbed a bottle of Coke, and pressed the cool glass against her bruised arm.

Dawn began remembering the beatings, the way Tucker ruled over her, a bipolar tyrant who dabbled in insanity.

"He didn't always used to be like this, Mom." Dawn found herself reliving the moments she tried to defend him. "We used to laugh and we were happy," she told her mom over a glass of lemonade.

"Well, I don't care how things used to be," her mother replied as she absently stroked Jimmy Bean in her lap. "You need to leave him."

"But he is a good man." Dawn began to cry. "He used to be so good. I don't know what happened to him. He's just so angry now. I don't know what came over him. It's like he's possessed."

"Dawn, listen," her mother said as she put the calico cat on the patio floor. "A good man would *never* lay his hands on a woman in anger." Her mother hung her head and began to sob. It pained Dawn to see her mother in this state. It simply broke her heart. "Every time I see you, you have a new bruise. You have got to get away from him," she sniffed. "He's a . . . a monster."

As Dawn slipped from one memory to another, she felt herself sliding further and further into darkness. Her memories began to fade into images she had never seen before. Instead of watching them from above, she felt as if she were physically in them. Monsters, black like oil, danced around her and flew above her, screeching. In the shadows stood a being, still as a statue, watching with red eyes as the others began pulling on her limbs, tearing off her clothes. She screamed as they savagely ripped the hair from her scalp. She awoke with a jolt, still screaming, and she almost fell off of the bed with Josiah still in her arms. She was drenched in shimmering blue sweat when she safely placed Josiah in the middle of the bed and pushed her wet hair off of her face.

Josiah was watching her curiously with his big eyes. She looked at him, wondering what he dreamt of, wondering if he remembered. Josiah sensed her unease and began to turn red as he wriggled his arms and scrunched his face.

"Oh, no, no, no, no!" Dawn tried to soothe him. "Shhhhhhhhhhh, shhhhhhhh, or do you want me to sing you a song?" Dawn threatened. She giggled at her joke, and he reciprocated her laugh with his own toothless baby chuckle. "Loving you is so easy." She sighed and smiled at the sight of his happy face and let the terrifying images fade into the crevices of her mind. He blinked at her and grabbed for his fat toes, cooing as she smiled down at him. Eventually Josiah fell back to sleep, leaving Dawn to watch him, envious. She watched as Josiah's fat tummy rose and fell and thought about turning him over. *Babies his age shouldn't sleep on their backs* she thought.

She caught herself slipping back into her mind. *But does that really matter here? We are all dead, so why do we even sleep at all?*

She lay there on her side, pondering their existence. She had been sitting in silence for so long, in a windowless room, that she didn't know if it was still night or if the sun had begun to rise. She found herself getting antsy as the unknown blanketed her thoughts. She shifted her weight, sighed, and shifted her weight again. She huffed loudly, stirring Josiah awake. She giggled when she saw his eyes open. He glanced at her, annoyed, as though he were just being woken from a sweet dream.

"Oops," she giggled again and then dug her nose into the fat rolls of his neck, tickling him and gently causing him to laugh loudly. They were startled by a heavy knocking on the door. Dawn had forgotten that they were not alone.

"Dawn," the unmistakable booming voice of Marlon came from the other side of the door. "Dawn, are you awake?"

"Come in," Dawn answered as she wrapped Josiah in his blanket and scooped him into her right arm. "Perfect fit," she whispered as Josiah's head sunk into place at her elbow. He reached a pudgy baby fist up to her face and kissed it long and hard before tucking it into the blanket.

"Good morning, Dawn," Marlon said as he opened the door and took one step in. "How did you sleep?"

"Not very well," she said, bending down to slip her feet into her white sneakers. "I had some nightmares. I guess I just don't get it," she said as she wiggled into the second shoe. "Why do I need sleep? I'm dead."

"You seem alive to me," Marlon smiled as he held out a lending hand to help her up from the bed. His body resembled a tree and his arm a thick, secure branch. "I know sometimes things can be hard to wrap your head around, but it's simple, really. All things that are energy need rest. You know, recharge the old batteries?"

"But," Dawn sighed.

"Dawn, I know you have a lot of questions, and that's why I'm here. I wanna show you around, make you feel comfortable, and get to know you a little too." The giant held the door open for Dawn as he ushered her out of the room. "You're one of us now. You're family, you and Joey.

"Before I begin the tour, I want to introduce you to one of your neighbors," Marlon said apprehensively. He stopped in the dank hallway and turned to Dawn. "Only if you want to, though."

"Um, okay," Dawn said quietly, not sure what she was agreeing to.

"Oh, she's just SO beautiful!" A boisterous female voice came from the hallway. Dawn looked confused for a moment, not sure from which door the short round woman came from. Marlon smiled, as the woman seemed to dance closer. Her short brown locks bounced with each step she took.

"This is Maribelle." Marlon gestured toward the woman. "Maribelle, this is Dawn."

"I can't believe you have been in this realm for three days and I am just now getting to say hello. Please excuse me! There is just so much madness going on! Everyone is bubbling with the news of the . . ."

"WELL," Marlon coughed and interrupted the sweet-faced woman. "Dawn and I really have a lot to do today, and well . . ." Marlon said uneasily.

"Is that the baby?" Maribelle squeaked, placing her dainty hands on her flushed cheeks. "Oh, may I please see him? Please?"

She was bouncing up and down in front of Dawn. There was something about this woman that gave Dawn a warm feeling inside. She was normal and felt common. Her responses and her actions and her movement reminded Dawn of women back home. Maribelle felt real.

"Oh, yes," Dawn said shyly as she bent down some so Maribelle could see. Josiah smiled at the new face and stretched out a hand he had managed to wiggle free from the wrap. The woman was now eagerly hanging on Dawn's forearm, pulling her down, begging to get a better look.

"Oh, my! What a beautiful baby!" She cooed in his face and Josiah cooed back. He now had both arms stretched out. His chubby baby fingers wiggled as they reached for Maribelle. Dawn smiled and held back a tear. The connection that she was witnessing between the two felt pleasantly familiar. Josiah was reaching for Maribelle the same way he used to reach for her mother. "May I hold him?" Maribelle asked, her passionate brown eyes searching Dawn's face.

"Oh, um, yes," Dawn answered reluctantly. "Yes, of course!" It was an awkward feeling handing Josiah over to Maribelle. Dawn had been the only one holding him for so long. In fact, Josiah had only ever really been held by Dawn and her mother.

With Josiah tucked securely in her arms, Maribelle began to dance. She twirled on her little feet, sending her pink dress rushing after her. Dawn watched in awe as Maribelle danced gracefully to the music only she could hear. She dipped and swayed and danced on her toes. All the while, Josiah was gurgling happily. When she finished and came off her pointed feet, Maribelle dug her nose into Josiah's chest and they both broke out in the sweetest laughter any of them had heard in a long while.

Marlon gently touched Dawn's shoulder. "I was hoping that we could just go and . . ." he hesitated before finishing his sentence.

"Yes," Dawn looked over her shoulder and into his dark eyes, "it's okay."

Marlon's composure immediately changed as he exhaled, "Oh good! I was so worried! I didn't know how you would respond and . . ."

"Marlon, it's okay," she shrugged. "We won't be going far," her eyes darted nervously from Marlon to Josiah, "right?"

"I will be right here in my room the whole time!" Maribelle sang. "We aren't going anywhere, are we, Joey?"

Dawn kissed the smiling baby goodbye and walked the opposite way down the earthen hallway. She had a hard time figuring out what to do with her hands, so she just shoved them into the little pockets of her brown capris. Marlon threw his big arm around her shoulders and embraced her as they simultaneously walked further into the earth.

"You're a very strong person, Dawn." He smiled at her and kissed her on the top of her head. Dawn smiled. *Family*, she thought.

Marlon gave Dawn a tour of the village. He explained to her that the cabins were simply the entrances to different parts of the village. The village itself was actually located underground. There were more openings leading to different parts of the forest that could only be seen by the person leaving them. Dawn refused to interrupt the giant as he spoke. Finally, some of her questions were being answered.

She marveled at how softly the giant spoke, how fluid his motions were. She felt close to him; she felt like she could trust him, even more than the others. Ulrica always seemed to be holding back, and Bancroft, though caring as he was, was rather aloof and disconnected at times. There was a sort of warmth that radiated from this giant. She wasn't sure if she was making that up or if it were true. *Family*, Dawn thought. *He feels like family.*

"So, our underground city, does it have a name?" she asked as the giant was showing her one of the back exits.

Marlon raised his boulder-sized knuckles and tapped a sequence on an aged wooden door. It magically swung open, allowing light to wash over them. He stepped back and gave Dawn the lead as they walked out into the open.

The cool, fresh air hit Dawn's body, stopping her clean in her tracks. She let the wind blow her long hair over her shoulder. Marlon stood behind her, waiting patiently, smiling as he watched her raise her head toward the sky and stretch her arms out by her sides. The sun, shimmering through the elm and oak leaves, felt warm on her cool face. The fresh breeze blew past her, stripping her of the underground stench. She stood and let the forest penetrate her senses. When she finally opened her eyes, she beheld the different shades of green that lit her surroundings. There were immense maple, birch, and elm trees that shot into the sky like skyscrapers. *Had the trees always been this big?* she thought. In the middle of it all was a bald opening; worn circles in the thick emerald grass surrounded the bases of the trees. Under one particularly large oak tree stood a big graying boulder.

Dawn turned to Marlon, smiling. When she saw the giant standing in the opening of a huge oak tree, her delicate mouth hung open and her arms fell to her sides. She looked past him and was astonished that she could clearly see the tunnel behind him. *A secret opening* she thought.

"Welcome to Middle Haven," Marlon whispered as he stepped closer to her. He watched her mouth drop in astonishment as the entrance disappeared behind him. He walked past her and took a seat below the towering oak tree. She was amazed at how easily the oak dwarfed the giant.

Dawn walked over to the sitting ground; the emerald-green grass felt soft and lush under her feet, as though she were walking on a mattress. She sat on a flat grey rock facing Marlon, who leaned against the tree with his legs crossed.

"That was amazing!" Dawn leaned forward with her elbows on her knees, cradling her petite chin in her hands, eager to learn more. Marlon leaned forward, squaring his elbows on his knees, smiling at her curiosity.

"Is there an Upper or Lower Haven?" she asked, leaning her body even closer to Marlon, hungry for more of the knowledge he had been feeding her.

"Not anymore." Marlon's disposition changed as he leaned his back against the tree once more. "There used to be." He looked wearily into the woods and started telling his story. "Before the treaties, we had large communities set up everywhere. Trick Point, Souls Bucket." He counted the places on his fingers. "Misty Bay," he chuckled, "also known as Itchy Trigger Bay."

He paused as he remembered, laying his head against the bark of the tree and closing his eyes as a tender breeze blew past them. In the sunlight, his skin looked radiant and reminded Dawn of the days she used to melt caramel to make snacks for the church.

He frowned as he opened his eyes. "We had so many nice villages and towns when the world was still good." He looked into Dawn's angelic face and feigned a smile. "But the world is no longer full of good. The evil spread like wildfire, and more and more tainted souls got stuck in this realm. We couldn't save them all." He snuffed and held out his large, empty hands. "We couldn't reach them all." He looked away from Dawn, whose gaze didn't falter. "We were outnumbered. Too many lost souls. The evil kingdom was expanding at an alarming rate. We were used to just having to deal with one or two evil souls. Put a blade through them and be done with it.

"But that just wasn't the case anymore. The evil kingdom was growing, taking in whatever we couldn't get our hands on. And not everything we got our hands on was worth saving. Eventually, the quest for souls became a battle. Both sides knew that the more souls they had, the more powerful they were.

"Well, things just got out of hand. The battle for souls became an all-out war. The thirst for power began to set evil seeds deep into our own community. Families and friends were torn apart. If we weren't losing our loved ones to war, we lost them to the greed and hate that began manifesting in our own ranks.

"We were supposed to be here to do good works for heaven, for God, and instead, we began reveling in the same sins we left behind on earth."

Marlon swung his big head back around to look at Dawn, who was now staring at her shoes. The grass beneath them was littered with acorns and fallen twigs and leaves. Her head was bowed and her long hair fell onto her empty arms. Strands of the black silk took flight when the wind blew. She leaned forward and picked up an acorn and brought it to her face. Puzzled, she looked up into the branches of the tree that stretched out above her. She held the acorn in her hand for a second and marveled at how such a tiny, weightless thing could turn into something so monumental. Bringing her attention back to Marlon, she brushed her hair back over her shoulder.

"So, when did the treaties come into place?" asked Dawn.

Marlon took a deep breath and turned his direction back to the woods. "The fighting had gotten so bad that high-level angels and demons were coming into the realm. And let me tell you." He turned to look Dawn in the face. "You don't wanna see these boys fight! They are powerful and their damage is permanent. Everything began spiraling out of control. So many innocent souls were lost forever. Both sides realized that they were fighting a losing battle. The realm was divided down the middle, and that's where we are today."

Dawn chewed on the information for a minute as she began digging a small hole in front of her with her fingers. She gently dropped the acorn into the dirt and wiped her hands on the sides of her pants, leaving dark-brown streaks on her otherwise clean capris.

"So there is the Frontier, Middle Haven, and then?" she asked, meeting Marlon's strong, dark eyes. He smiled at her and began picking smaller rocks out of the earth, getting rich, black earth under his clean fingernails.

"There are a few more small communities," he started, as he began placing the rocks around Dawn's buried acorn, "but the next big one is called Little Heaven."

"What's heaven like?" Dawn asked in a quiet voice, now focused solely on Marlon.

Marlon shifted his weight and looked onto her porcelain face. He gently lifted the stubborn lock of hair that always seemed to be dangling in the way of her beauty and tucked it behind her ear.

"It's *everything* you ever dreamed it would be." For a moment's time, Dawn felt lost in his gaze—not the scared, worried lost she was used to, but a warm, free lost that made her feel like flying. Dawn broke her gaze and the couple looked shyly about themselves.

"So, why come back here?" Dawn asked. It seemed simple enough to Dawn that if one were perfectly happy in one place, then why leave.

The giant smiled his patient smile and gently replied, "Just because you're in heaven doesn't mean you no longer have a conscience or feelings. It's the most perfect place to be. In the beginning, you do whatever it is your heart desires. But you eventually begin to wonder how your family is doing. How your friends are doing. How the world is doing." He sighed. "And eventually, you look down and see that things on earth are horrible. So, it's only natural that you would want to lend a hand. So, you get yourself stationed to a post in the middle realm so you can help, as a Beacon, like Ulrica and Bancroft, or a solider, or, well, whatever you wanna be."

"Why not go to earth and help directly?"

"Only angels have that power." Marlon started to get up. Dawn put her hand on his forearm.

"Thank you."

He simply smiled his flawless smile and rose. From Dawn's position on the rock, he seemed to shoot up like a tree. His large frame cast a shadow over her. "We'd better get back inside. It's never a good idea to stay out here too long. Especially nowadays." He gestured a hand toward Dawn, and she grabbed it and allowed herself to be helped up. She followed the giant, with a heavy heart, to the tree where he tapped a special knock and they, once again, entered the underground village.

Chapter 8

Seeds of Mistrust

*T*he following morning, after a turbulent night filled with nightmares and more nightmares, Bancroft came to pick up Dawn. Together, they dropped Josiah off at Maribelle's, who was all smiles when she saw them, and followed the tunnels to the west side and headed out to the sparring grounds. Marlon and Ulrica where already waiting for them, practicing their aim by throwing hatchets at tree stumps that had targets etched into them.

"Today we are going to teach you how to throw a hatchet!" Bancroft beamed enthusiastically. The first time Dawn threw it, she missed the target by five feet, losing her hatchet in the woods. After ten other failed attempts, an impatient Ulrica decided to show her the art of the bow and arrow, one of Ulrica's specialties. Ulrica's heritage was still strong in her soul, and many times she spoke in her native tongue as she was instructing Dawn. Ulrica seemed to float around Dawn as she told her how to bend her elbow and straighten her back. She whispered in Dawn's ear, revealing the secrets of the pull back and the release.

Despite her tender lessons, the skills of archery also eluded Dawn. She pulled back the bow and almost hit her own foot with the arrow! Bancroft fell to the ground laughing. Ulrica carefully took the bow away from Dawn, who spotted silver sweat beads on Ulrica's forehead as she manually released Dawn's fingers from the bow.

"You're probably the first person to ever come so close to killing yourself with your own bow and arrow!" Bancroft rolled on the emerald grass as his laughter filled the sparring grounds. Dawn's embarrassment grew when she looked about her and realized that everyone was laughing. When she looked over to Ulrica and saw her laughing as well, Dawn smiled sheepishly and realized Bancroft was probably right.

"So, what's next?" Dawn said, standing awkwardly in the middle, laughing at herself.

After little deliberation, Marlon, Ulrica, and Bancroft decided to train Dawn on close combat.

"It's not like we are ever going to be leaving her alone anyway," Bancroft said. Bancroft and Ulrica began teaching Dawn defensive techniques. Marlon left to spar with two tall black men in overalls. Ulrica and Bancroft had Dawn train all morning long. Dawn felt more empowered with each new move she learned.

By the time Marlon came back to check on their progress, the sun had moved to its peak.

"So, how's it going?" he inquired.

"Good," Dawn replied, with her head locked in Ulrica's arm. The two had progressed to ground work.

"Good," Marlon smiled, looking down on the couple. "Then I guess we should test your skills." Marlon looked around the sparring grounds as Ulrica helped Dawn up off the ground, patting her on her back, before dusting herself off. Marlon spotted two red-headed women relaxing under an elm.

"Kelly, Shannon!" he called out to them. They immediately popped up and ran over to Marlon and the others. "Is one of you free to be a sparring partner?" Kelly, the older sister, looked at Dawn and raised an eyebrow.

"No, sorry," she said unapologetically as she cut her eyes. "I'm extremely busy." She looked the other way to a blonde man with a crooked nose who had just entered the grounds out of an oak tree. "Emitt!" she yelled and ran to the man with no further explanation, her long red hair flying loose behind her.

Shannon looked at Dawn and smiled shyly. Her apple-shaped

face was framed by her straight bangs and cropped fire-red hair. Her round cheeks were sprinkled with freckles, like cinnamon on top of the fluffed milk of a cappuccino. She held out a slender, freckled arm. "Hi! I'm Shannon! Nice to meet you. Sorry about my sister." She smiled at Dawn, and her friendly green eyes sparkled.

"Take it easy on her, this was her first day." Bancroft wagged his finger like an overprotective mother. *Family*, Dawn thought, smiling sweetly in his direction. Dawn and Shannon stood in the middle of the group, hands in front of their faces in a defensive stance, circling each other, both too timid to throw the first blow.

"Well, someone is going to have to advance," Ulrica pointed out, standing bored with her arms crossed in front of her.

Kelly and her boyfriend came strolling up to the group. Kelly stood in front of Emitt, who was taller than her, and rested his sharp chin on her head. He held her around her waist, and she held his arms tight to her and leaned in to support body.

"Aww, come on!" Kelly yelled to her sister, "What are you waiting for? Attack already!"

With the arrival of her coach, Shannon lurched forward, attempting to punch Dawn in her body. Dawn saw the swing coming and grabbed her arm. She pulled Shannon closer and immediately put her into a headlock. Ulrica smiled and Bancroft beamed. Marlon tried to hide his excitement.

"Are you serious?" Kelly yelled, no longer in Emitt's embrace. "I'm outta here!" She stomped away, grabbing Emitt's hand on her way to the shade of an elm tree.

The two sparred until the sun began to set. Shannon's short red hair turned a shimmery brown with sweat.

"You're not so bad!" Shannon said in a sweet voice, smiling at Dawn. She was half a head shorter than Dawn, but they shared the same willowy frame.

"You weren't just playing it easy, were you?" Dawn asked as they started walking toward the tree.

Shannon chuckled as she wiped the sweat from her face. "What, you think I like being put in headlocks?" They both laughed as they entered the underground tunnels. "Same time tomorrow?" Dawn nodded and smiled back.

"Thank you, thank you so much!" Dawn said before heading to Maribelle's to pick up Josiah for the night.

The next morning, the two sparring women drew a crowd. Dawn surprised everyone with her agility in sparring. They sparred until midday, then Marlon and Ulrica decided to entrust Dawn with two wooden daggers and replaced Shannon with Emitt. Emitt also held two wooden daggers and was standing in front of her with a cocky smile. He flipped his blonde hair back and glared at Dawn; she knew she was weaker than he was. As she stood across from him, she flashed back to her old life. Tucker used to smile like that. Her mind began to race with fear. Emitt's face flashed to Tucker's, only to flash back to Emitt's. Marlon came up from behind and touched her shoulder, startling her so deeply that she dropped her daggers. She spun around and fell into Marlon's broad chest, burying her tears in his shirt. She was embarrassed and scared and surrounded by half the town.

"Hey, heeeey," Marlon soothed her, his palm stretched out, embracing her upper back. "What just happened?" As he whispered into her ear through her black locks, he could feel her tears through his shirt.

"Muammmer." Her voice was muffled and the words unrecognizable.

"All right, everyone. Show's over," Bancroft yelled to crowd. "Go on!" He was the shortest person there and his face was stern. "Get!" He shooed the crowd away until the only people remaining were Ulrica, Emitt, Dawn, and Marlon.

"Hey," Marlon whispered. "They are all gone." He took his massive hands and placed them on Dawn's shoulders. She hung her head and allowed him to gently push her away from his chest.

"What's the matter, Dawn?" Marlon asked, adding his hands to her shoulders. Dawn wiped her eyes and felt yet another hand rest on her shoulder.

"Dawn," Ulrica said from her side, "you have nothing to fear. We are all here." The hands on her shoulders should have felt heavy, yet Dawn felt her head rise and her back straighten.

"I . . . it's . . . Tucker," Dawn managed to stutter before she felt her eyes raise to look into Marlon's brown face. "He reminded me of Tucker. I saw his face flash and . . ."

Ulrica's hand slid off her shoulder and down her arm. Ulrica's hand was soft but firm, and Dawn felt her fingers intertwine with her own. She squeezed lightly until Dawn turned to face her.

"You need to fight this man," Ulrica said, pointing over to Emitt who was still standing, holding the two wooden daggers. He was no longer sneering; his blue eyes looked deeply concerned.

"Was it something I did?" he asked, taking a step closer to Dawn, who quickly looked away, down to her feet.

"Look at him!" Ulrica squeezed her hand tightly now.

The hands on Dawn's shoulders pressed harder, and she raised her head and looked into Ulrica's strong face. Dawn felt empowered, supported, by the hands that seemed to hold her up. She dared another look behind her to Emitt, who hadn't moved.

"Face your fear," Ulrica said firmly before squeezing her hand one more time and then releasing it. Ulrica backed up, and then Dawn felt the hands lift off her shoulders. She turned and faced Emitt, who was now daggerless.

"I'm sorry," Dawn's voice creaked.

"Don't be sorry," Ulrica snapped. "Pick up your daggers, both of you!"

Dawn and Emitt reluctantly bent down and picked up their wooden daggers. "Now, hold them up! Both of you!" They obeyed. She stood in between the two, her arms stretched out and her long, cotton skirt swayed in the breeze. Two thick braids hung down her front. "Now, Emitt, come and attack Dawn." Emitt inched forward. "Like you mean it!" Ulrica screeched.

Dawn watched Emitt step closer and closed her eyes.

"Open them!" Ulrica yelled. "You watch him come close, you look for the anger in his eyes." Dawn opened her eyes, visibly shaken. "Look at him!" Ulrica ordered. "He's a big, strong man, and he has weapons. And he wants to hurt you!"

"Not helping," Dawn whispered through gritted teeth. As she watched Emitt approach, the look of concern had washed from his face. He now approached her ominously, his hair hanging in front of his face, covering his grey eyes.

"You will fight this man." Ulrica was no longer yelling. Her voice was stern and her finger pointed at Emitt. The beads of her turquoise bracelet chimed with the clinking of her beaded belt. "There are beings out there that want to hurt you!" Emitt stepped closer, and Dawn watched as his white fists tightened around the handle of his weapons. She began to back up on legs that were wobbling like cooked spaghetti.

"No." Marlon's voice was a deep wall that pushed her forward.

"They are out in that forest." Ulrica continued. "They will take you, hurt you, make you disappear forever." Emitt had come close enough to Dawn to reach out and touch her. "Now, think of Joey."

Without another thought, Dawn leaped forward into Emitt's chest, throwing him onto his back, and landing with her knees straddling Emitt's waist. Her daggers stabbed the ground at the sides of Emitt's head.

"WOOOOO! Thata girl!" Bancroft shouted as he jumped around. Marlon laughed with his arms crossed over his chest. His voice boomed into the forest.

Ulrica let a smile escape her lips. "Now, do it again!"

After sparring well into the evening with Emitt, it was evident that Dawn had found her strength. She felt powerful and strong for the first time in her life.

Afterward, Bancroft took her for a walk. He explained that everyone has the power to fight, the power to stand up and fight inside of them. "It's primal." She was a close-combat warrior. Dawn could only think how absurd that sounded. She remembered the beatings she had endured by Tucker's hands. Where were her instincts then? But still, it was nice to see Bancroft grinning proudly from ear to ear, pleased with her performance. Ulrica smiled too, not as big or as bright, but she smiled.

That night Dawn felt like a new woman lying in her bed next to Josiah. Despite the empowering last couple of days, Dawn's nights had continued to be erratic and sleepless. She wondered if the dead could dream, because she surely was not. When she did finally sleep, her nights were filled with nightmares, sadness, anger, and perpetual loss. Eerie, dark beasts and shrill screams woke her every night, leaving her soaked in silver tears, with wet hair matted to her face. How long had she been crying? Would she ever forget her former life and all its pain?

"Maybe it would be easier to be a sliver," Dawn whispered to herself in the darkness.

The following morning, after once again giving up on sleep, Dawn decided to skip her training. She silently made her way through the halls in the early-morning hours, with Josiah in her arms. She wondered if this rich earth smell would penetrate her and if she would start smelling like dirt. She dug her nose into Josiah's neck fat. He still smelled like a baby. She looked behind her in the hall, and after confirming that no one was behind her, she lifted Josiah into the air and smelled her own underarms. To her surprise and relief, she smelled of dry blossoms, the scent of her deodorant.

As she passed her sitter's door, she wondered how long it would take for the others to notice her absence. *What are they gonna do, ground me?* Dawn smiled to herself at her little pun. She had never been the joking kind, always forgetting the punch line and mixing the blondes with the brunettes. People usually laughed more at her mistakes than the actual joke.

She began to pick up her pace as she made her way back to the meeting place on the east side where Marlon had brought her a few days before. It is cool under the earth. It feels safe, but there are no windows, and there is no sun and no air. She desperately wanted to lie in the grass and not worry about counter blocks and what the others were thinking. She needed to feel the glorious sun and let her hair blow in the fresh breeze. It made her feel human; it made her feel worthy. The warmth seemed to help her remember who she is, not what she was.

With Josiah in one hand, she rapped on the dark wooden door, hoping it was the right one. It took only a gentle brush of the fingertips to open the large door, and she gracefully stepped out of the earth through an immense oak. She immediately turned her head toward the bright morning sky as the wind blew her hair in all directions around her. She smiled as the refreshing air flowed through her clothes and whipped her hair. She felt like dancing, laughing, or making a wish she knew would never come true. Feeling free and uplifted, she smiled down at Josiah's squinting face.

"Oh, poor baby." She smiled and used her hand to shield his eyes from the daylight. "Let me go find us a nice spot in the shade."

Dawn chose a lush spot under the same ancient oak she shared with Marlon. She glanced over to the acorn she planted just days before and wondered how it could be that trees and plants grew and lived in this realm. She pondered over much as she lay in the grass with Josiah. It was good to get away from the others, she thought as she tickled her nose with a bright-yellow dandelion. She always felt as though someone were keeping things from her. *What is it they don't want me to know?* Dawn looked at the yellow dandelion she held in her hand. She stopped moving when she saw the tips of her fingers were shimmering with the silver juice that came out of the flower. She squeezed the stem of the dandelion, and a drop of liquid silver fell onto her neck. The wind blew hard, and Josiah giggled as the strong breeze washed her black locks over his face. Having her attention broken, she tossed the dandelion to the side and devoted herself to Josiah.

"Oh, you like that huh?" Dawn turned onto her side and took the strand of hair Josiah loved so much and tickled him with it. "How about if I get your fat little baby toes?" She giggled as she pretended to eat his feet. She loved this child more than anything in the world. She knew she would do anything for him at anytime, anywhere.

As she was marveling at how his laugh seemed to echo in her heart, a shadow overcame them.

"You know, you really shouldn't be out here all alone." She looked up still smiling, only to see Jorge. Her demeanor immediately changed, her smile vanished. In an instant, Dawn was sitting up, cradling Josiah in her arms as though the beautiful morning had turned into a blustery winter day.

"Well, now, I'm not that unsightly, am I?" Jorge said with the corners of his mouth turned up.

Dawn did not want to seem rude for what she was about to say, so she apologized before replying.

"I'm sorry," she said as she tucked her hair behind her ears, "but are you smiling?"

"Oh, c'mon!" Jorge was clearly offended as he threw his skinny arms into the air. "Do you really think I'm that cold?"

Dawn raised her eyebrows as if to suggest the thought had crossed her mind.

"Well . . ." she began.

"Look," Jorge gestured with his hand, silently asking if it would be okay to take a seat next to Dawn in the shade. She nodded politely and even moved over a bit to make room for him. It was a completely unnecessary action, as there was so much grass under the immense oak tree that it would have been impossible not to have enough shade for the three of them. "I have to admit. I wasn't happy to see you here."

Dawn was well aware of that fact. She felt he had been quick to judge her. "You don't even know me."

"No, I don't. Let me explain." Jorge, sitting on the ground, shifted his weight and put his right palm up to show that he wanted the floor. "I, we, don't really like it when strangers come into our village surrounded in as much mystery as you two were." The wind blew hard again, causing leaves to believe in flight, only to come floating down again.

"We?" Dawn asked, looking into his pale face.

"Well, my wife and my friends, others. Well, almost everyone who isn't the giant or the two you came in with," he replied, almost straining to keep his thin smile on his face.

"What mystery?" Dawn thought she might have a clue as to what Jorge was talking about, but wanted him to clarify.

Jorge questioned in honest surprise, "Really? You haven't heard the rumors?"

Now he really had her attention. He watched as her hair flew about her. Her full lips quivered and her eyes glowed like sapphires, ablaze with questions. Dawn's thirst for answers grew fierce, and he enjoyed watching the transformation.

"Well, for one, you came in under the protection of a phoenix. You do know he's not allowed this far down, right?"

"Yeah, I learned that. From you," she replied. "What rumors?"

Jorge smiled a sinister smile, knowing he had her hooked. "Well, I don't want to make you feel awkward or even hurt," he looked into Dawn's hungry eyes and waited for her to beg.

"Please, tell me!" Dawn pleaded. "It's in my best interest to know what everyone thinks about me."

"Well, I guess by now you know that not everyone thinks you're as special as Bancroft does. With them thinking you're the Second Coming and all."

"Second what?" Dawn was flabbergasted. "The Second Coming? Me?" Dawn didn't know much about the Second Coming, only that it was supposed to be Jesus. Looking at Jorge, she began to distrust his friendliness. The wind had died down, and the sound of rustling of leaves gave way to her thoughts.

Where are the others? Why send Jorge? I never talk to him. Why is he here? Was he waiting for me to be alone? He's not my friend.

"How stupid do you think I am, Jorge?" she asked him with her face cut cold as stone.

Jorge was taken aback by her question. He squirmed uncomfortably as he felt the control of the conversation slip.

"What?"

"Me? The Second Coming?" Jorge sat quietly and pursed his lips. He looked from her anxious eyes to Josiah and back into her eyes again. Dawn broke his gaze and looked into the direction of the wind. She closed her eyes as she held back the tears. She began to realize who the phoenix broke the treaty for, who he really came to protect. "Let me ask you a question," Dawn said as the wind died down again. She raised her head and straightened her back as she looked directly into Jorge's cold dark eyes. "If I would have died in the woods alone, would I have found the cabin?"

Jorge had originally set out to hurt this young woman, and now he felt bad because he knew he would.

"No." Jorge looked away from her and hung his shoulders, knowing the damage had been done.

"I see." Dawn looked over at Jorge, who was staring into the woods. When he turned back to face her, his thin lips formed a frown and his eyes looked sad and apologetic. His thin nose flared as he searched for a way to take the pain away. His pale face was distraught with the conversation that had gone his way, but hadn't. "Could you take Joey inside, please? I need some time to breathe." Before this conversation, Dawn wouldn't have left Josiah alone with Jorge, not for one hundred sunny days. Now she knew it wasn't her that gave Josiah protection. Alas, it was the other way around. He had been protecting her.

"Sure." Jorge took Josiah into his arms. "He really is a beautiful baby." Jorge smiled at him as though lost in some side world.

"Yeah, he is," Dawn whispered.

"I'll take him inside now." Jorge had a different tone. It was almost as though holding the baby made his entire shell glow. He walked lighter; he almost skipped to the underground entrance.

"I'll be there in a minute," Dawn said, trying to usher Jorge away from her.

"I will wait right here until you're ready to come in," he said as he leaned against the tree, cuddling Josiah and cooing at him, touching his pointy nose to Josiah's button nose. "I can't leave you out here by yourself," Jorge sang as he gently bounced Josiah in his arms.

Dawn sat in the grass, petting it with her hands, letting the stubby ends tickle her palms. *Who am I?* she thought. She looked over at Jorge, who was singing some kind of song in a language that sounded vaguely familiar. She fought back the tears. *Why am I?*

That night Joey was restless; perhaps he felt Dawn's apprehensions. Either way, they were both awake in their tiny room, which began to feel more and more like a clay prison. Dawn slipped on her shoes, ran her fingers through her hair, wrapped Josiah in a blanket, and exited the room. She decided that she already knew what was to the right, so she turned left, ready to explore this side of the hallway, which happened to be a whole lot like the other side: narrow and dirty. The candles led the way past this door on the right and that door on the left. As Dawn passed the door leading to the meeting grounds, she began to wonder who on earth would dig such a boring tunnel. She threw a glance over her shoulder, just to make sure the hallway was still behind her. It was. She frowned. *Really,* she thought to herself, *I never thought I'd be bored in the afterlife.* It was true. It might have been boring, definitely repetitive, but she was moving, and that beat lying in bed, listening to herself think. At any rate, Josiah seemed to be happier, and he had finally fallen asleep. Dawn sighed and whispered, "Well, I guess it's time to turn around.

At least one of us is happy."

It was then that a thudding caused Dawn to peer further into the hallway. She saw a slender beam of light sneaking its way up the hallway floor. Someone left a door open. Quiet as a mouse, she inched closer to the door. People were arguing back and forth, but Dawn couldn't make out the words until she heard her name. She had reached the door on the right and made herself flat against the wall next to it, taking a quick second to check the baby, who was still fast asleep in her arms. Dawn rested her head against the wall, so close to the wooden door frame she could feel the splinters threatening to penetrate the soft flesh of her ear.

"YOU TOLD HER WHAT?" Bancroft roared.

"I thought she already knew." Jorge's voice was relaxed and cool.

"But why? Why would you tell her that? The way she must feel right now!" Bancroft pleaded with Jorge as if the words had not already been spoken. Dawn didn't need to look into the room to know that Bancroft was pacing the floor, huffing his pipe.

"We all have pain, Bancroft." The voice was so calm and in control it could only have been Ulrica's.

"Or have you forgotten all of your sacrifices, little man?" Jorge added. That Ulrica and Jorge were in agreement only confused Dawn. The whole time here at Middle Haven they either argued or avoided one another.

"Oh, so now you wanna side with him?" Bancroft said angrily. Dawn had never heard him speak that way to Ulrica. "Dammit!" Something hit the wall and rattled onto the floor in front of the door, scaring the breath out of Dawn. "She's a good girl!"

"No one is saying otherwise," Ulrica said calmly. "The bottom line is she might get in the way."

"We have the *world* to think about," Jorge added.

"You guys think you can right your wrongs," Bancroft spat. "You can't! You think you will be redeeming yourselves! You can't!

You have already been forgiven!" Bancroft yelled.

"Bancroft, dear, please sit." Dawn could hear Ulrica pull the chair out for her husband.

"Listen to me and my . . ." Ulrica began. "Someone's coming."

Dawn fled down the hall to her room. She had heard enough anyway. Once in the confines of her room, she sobbed, waking Josiah. She looked into his innocent face; he was completely unaware of the burdens his shoulders were meant to bear. She remembered the fate Jesus had. After all his amazing works, he was tortured, nailed to a cross, and left to die. Was this the fate of her love, of her Josiah? She stroked his fluffy baby hairs as she cried for him. He blinked and cooed at her, but she didn't smile back. She couldn't smile back. Silver-blue scars marred her face as the tears fell onto his blanket.

I am just a pawn. The thought slammed her like a freight train. *I was just a pawn. I would have loved him and raised him and gone through all of the tribulations, freely and willingly.* Dawn kissed Josiah's soft forehead.

"And I still would, but you don't need me. No one needs me."

She looked around the room, her vision blurred from her weeping. She felt the walls close in on her, coming closer with each breath she took. She was suffocating.

Chapter 9

Run Away

Dawn exited the underground fortress, passed the common grounds, and tramped into the woods. She kept walking and walking, sure that someone would notice she had vanished, sure that someone would come and get her. Eventually, tears began to spill down her face as she realized no one missed her. Maribelle didn't even question her as Dawn left Josiah gurgling at her bosom.

As she walked through the forest, the moon provided a wonderful glow, making the forest look magical. Dawn failed to notice the nocturnal beauty. She was too depressed and angry. She knew there were dangers in the woods, but she was too hurt to concern herself with them. She no longer cared. *If they don't care, why should I?* she thought as she stepped over a fallen tree.

As the last of her tears rolled off her chin, she looked up and saw a glow in the forest off to her left. It was a dome of pale-blue light that stood alone amid the darkness. Curiosity willed her to go closer. Before long, she was standing at the foot of a beautiful orchard. It was a mini forest within the forest.

All of the trees were in bloom and were absolutely radiant in the moonlight. The dogwoods, with their short, skinny trunks, boasted heavenly white and lavender blossoms. The cherry trees stood majestically, their tops glowing a pale pink. Even the ground was littered in blossoms. There were strawberry patches, whose thick, green leaves were spotted with tiny white flowers that had yellow centers. Raspberry bushes were luminous in the moonlight; their bright pink and purple buds seemed to blush among the dark-green grass. Even the grass itself was aglow with buttercups. In the middle of it all stood a huge apple tree, with almost as many blossoms as stars in the sky. Its twisted, aged trunk dug deep into the ground.

This hidden forest was magical and hypnotizing. So hypnotizing, in fact, that Dawn couldn't remember what had made her so angry. She felt calm and at ease as she walked closer and closer to the apple tree that stood in the middle of everything. She stopped in front of it and marveled. Something moved over her foot, cool and dry. Dawn looked down to see a snake slithering by. She wasn't afraid or startled as she should have been, would have been. She simply walked up to the tree and sat underneath its massive branches. With her back against its sturdy and scratchy trunk, she looked up. Now it really did look like she was looking into the night sky. Between the dark branches, the light of the blossoms seemed to twinkle.

"God made everything so beautiful, just for you, Dawn," she remembered her mother saying. Dawn thought of her mother, and her body filled with warmth as she curled up under the twisted trunk of the tree. She took one last look about her and closed her eyes.

Despite her tranquil surroundings, Dawn's dreams were more turbulent and violent than ever. The peaceful bliss that dreams are supposed to be made of was ravaged with visions of souls being lost and taken by vicious monsters. There was so much pain, and war was all around her. So many spilled souls made it seem as though she were fighting in a lake. All of a sudden she was in the air being taken away, ripped away, from Josiah. Josiah was crying, screaming, and then she awoke with a start.

It was still night and the trees still glowed, but something was different. Something had changed. When it all had felt so peaceful before, it now felt dangerous.

"I am watching you."

Dawn sat up straight and looked around. She knew she was no longer alone. Then she saw him, standing with his back to her in the moonlight that shone through a gaping hole in the trees. Dawn was startled but still not afraid. The wind began to rustle through the trees, causing a beautiful cloud of pastel leaves and petals to float about her. The leaves fell so thick that Dawn could no longer see the man. She became mesmerized by the falling petals; never in her life had she had the privilege to witness a scene this strikingly beautiful. She forgot the man, she forgot how to fear. Dawn stood perfectly still in the gentle storm of leaves that rained down around her. The wind died down and the last of the leaves began to silently fall to the ground, like snow on Christmas. The forest bed had been covered in a thick blanket of fallen petals. One brushed her cheek and another landed on her bare shoulder. Without looking, she brushed it off and began to wonder whether the man she saw was real or if she had still been dreaming. She took a step back and lost her footing on a root of the apple tree. In that instant, a hand reached out from behind and saved her from her fall. She spun around, nearly falling again, holding fast to the hand that saved her. Dawn found herself staring into darkness. She could barely make out a silhouette of a face in the shadow of the tree. Dawn took little steps back, and the man who held her hand took those same steps forward. As his face came out of the shadows, Dawn held her breath.

A more handsome face she had never seen. He was a good bit taller than her. His hair was long and dreadlocked, and his skin was brown like sugar. But it was his eyes that caught her attention: his dark coal eyes. The two stood there, staring into each other's eyes, not saying a word. Dawn didn't know what to say, and it seemed that her mysterious man didn't either. So there they stood in silence, holding hands.

Dawn took a breath to speak, but the man quickly covered her mouth with his free hand. He took his hand away as soon as he saw that she understood there was to be no speaking. He took Dawn by the waist and led her out of the glowing orchard and onto an open plateau. The handsome stranger took Dawn right to the edge of the cliff, and Dawn, feeling no fear in her heart, allowed him to pull her there. The view was phenomenal. At the edge of the cliff in the early-morning hours, Dawn was able to see what seemed like the entire ocean. The pale glow of the moon illuminated and accentuated every wave's curves and crests. She closed her eyes, smelled the salt of the ocean, and heard the sound of the waves crashing on the rocks below her. She lifted her head toward the sky and the moon reflected off of her face, making her look angelic and divine. Dawn opened her eyes and stared at the vast sky above. The stars were countless, and the moon dominated the sky. Had the night always been this beautiful? It was then that she no longer felt the hand around her waist. Dawn turned around and looked back at the man who had brought her here.

He was sitting back a bit on the grass, barefoot, leaning on his elbows, and looking straight up into the sky with a smile on his face. He almost seemed to be sunbathing in the moonlight. He was wearing a pair of thin beige pants that tied at his waist. He was shirtless, and his body looked as though it had been chiseled out of some brown foreign rock. Dawn stared because he was beautiful, but also because she couldn't remember whether or not he had a shirt on in the orchard. She could not remember. She could only remember his smoldering gaze, and with that thought, she looked back into his face.

"Who are you?" Dawn took a seat next to this shirtless stranger. He slowly opened his eyes and looked at her. For a moment, Dawn thought she saw a glimmer of red light in his dark eyes, but then he spoke.

"Kale be my name," he said. "What be yours?"

"Dawn." She didn't know what else to say. Was she love struck? She was well aware of the fact that she didn't know where she was, who she was with, and where all of this was leading. She just knew that she wasn't afraid.

Kale closed his eyes and then repeated her name in a whisper. "Mmmmm, Dawn. Very beautiful name." Dawn felt flushed, like a school child. "Beautiful name, beautiful girl." He took her hand in his, and they sat at the edge of the cliff looking out into the vast open space before them. Moments passed before Kale turned to Dawn's pale face again. "So, my lady, tell me your story."

"I'll tell you mine if you tell me yours."

Kale leaned in to bring his face closer to hers. Her eyes sparkled in the night's light, and he couldn't seem to figure out what made her so special. "I promise." He paused, still staring into her eyes, and then put a hand up to her cheek and rubbed his thumb along her cheekbone. "If you want, I will tell you mine first."

Dawn shied away from his gaze that took her prisoner and focused on the grass. "No, that's okay. I'll take your word. So, where should I begin."

"How much do you remember?" Kale's eyes flashed red again, and this time, Dawn was sure she wasn't seeing things.

Dawn began to tell her story. Kale listened intently, as did everyone who she told the story to. She didn't hesitate to tell Kale about Josiah and who the others think he is. By the end of her story, she lay in Kale's arms, her head resting on his chest, and his fingers combing through her thick hair.

"Josiah . . ." Kale said, letting the name resound in the air around them. "Well, then, the rumors are true." Kale was talking aloud to himself.

Dawn rose from his chest, her hair rippled down from the top of her head and hung freely over her shoulders. "Who are you?" Again, she saw the red in his eyes.

"My name is Kale." He looked behind them as if to check for others and then continued speaking. "I'm an enemy to those you left behind. I'm a fierce warrior. But I am also a fierce lover."

Dawn shifted her weight uncomfortably as he finished his last sentence. "No, you misunderstand." He smiled a sheepish grin, flashing his white teeth. "I, like every being in existence, have good and evil in me. I can be full of hate, but I can also be full with love."

He looked at Dawn as he tried to explain. "I am a fierce warrior, yes." He struggled with his words. "But I am also capable of loving, just as hard and deep as everyone else." He paused. "We all are."

"*What* are you?" Dawn asked carefully, keeping her gaze on him.

"You must understand. I mean you no harm. Especially now that I have heard your story." Kale broke his gaze and lowered his head. He seemed ashamed, but more than that, he was scared.

Dawn knew she wouldn't want to hear what Kale had to say. She had a gut-wrenching feeling that she was about to get hurt. Not a slap on the face kind of hurt, but a thump to the heart. She looked away from Kale's pleading face and into the now bright-orange sky. The sun was beginning to rise; the purples and oranges and reds seemed to push the darkness into the other direction.

"The dawn is always fighting the night. It's an endless battle that can never be won, just as twilight will always triumph over day." Kale, too, was marveling at the transformation above them. He held onto Dawn's hand but purposely kept his gaze to the skies. He didn't want to see her reaction.

Such a beautiful view. Such a wonderful and intriguing night. But as Dawn already knew, all good things must come to an end.

"Kale," she looked at him and with her free hand gently turned his head to face hers, "you promised."

"I'm a Gidly," he whispered and then flinched, clearly expecting Dawn to jerk back and scream. "I've been watching you for some time now." He rattled and wanted to get all of his information out before she could speak and leave him. "That first night at your basement window, I was on orders to collect you and," he hesitated, "and the baby."

Dawn shot him a deadly look after mentioning Josiah. So he hurriedly finished, "The night I saw you, I knew I would never harm you. I broke ranks and never returned to my camp. I followed you, watching you, waiting for the right moment to confront you. I didn't expect to find you in the garden. When I saw you, I knew I had to say something."

Dawn said nothing. "Well, you have me now. What is it you wanted?"

"I don't know."

Dawn stood up and walked to the edge of the cliff. The sun was now bright, and she smiled at the warmth it gave her. She turned around and saw Kale getting up. He faced her, and she smiled at him as he approached her. Dawn reached her hand to his face, but before she could touch him, he jerked his head to the right and looked over his shoulder. "They are coming for you!"

Dawn's eyes grew wide with fear. "Who?" She had forgotten that they were not the only two souls in this realm.

"Your people." Kale turned to run, but Dawn held his arm close to her body. "You need to know that there is good and evil in every being. Please remember this."

Kale pulled Dawn in and their lips sealed. The kiss seemed to last forever, and when it was done, it left Dawn wanting more.

"Wait, where are you going?" She knew she would have to say goodbye but couldn't let go. "I don't want you to leave me!"

"Then I won't." With those words, Kale took her head in both his hands and kissed her swiftly goodbye. He turned and took off in the woods in the opposite direction.

"I'm watching you."

Dawn placed her fingers over her lips, smiled, and said, "I'll be missing you." She turned around and sat at the edge of the cliff, taking in the fresh salt air, the warm sun, and the crashing sounds. She thought of Kale and his perfect kiss and waited for them to come find her.

Chapter 10

Grounded

*T*here they came, the four of them, storming out of the forest. Ulrica, Bancroft, Jorge, and Marlon were armed and dangerous. *Who would ever be stupid enough to attack them?* Dawn wondered as she stood and dusted herself off. Bancroft was the first to spot Dawn and pointed the way with his broad ax. Upon seeing his face, she immediately felt ashamed. Directly behind him, Marlon, full of anger, came bursting through the forest, knocking down a small tree with his morning star. For the first time since Dawn had left the village, she felt fear. Raw fear.

Dawn saw Ulrica and Jorge, both blatantly annoyed, walking side by side behind Marlon and Bancroft, who were now racing toward her. They both held their weapons with a sense of indifference and were not really trying to catch up.

"What in the hell are you doing way out here?" Marlon's voice boomed. "Do you know how dangerous *this* is?" Marlon reached Dawn first, and out of his grief, picked her up and threw her slender shell over his shoulder like a sack of socks. Marlon immediately started marching back in the direction from which they had come. Dawn propped her body up with her elbows on his broad back and watched as the others trailed behind her.

"You could have been killed!" Marlon shouted.

"You had us worried to death!" Bancroft looked up at her face. His round bald head was spotted with shiny blue balls of sweat and his eyes were wet with worry. It was the same look Dawn's mother had given her after each of Tucker's beatings: relived she was alive but worried still.

"Yes, we were so worried," Ulrica chimed in with the emotions of a robot.

Bancroft, now out of breath from trying to keep up with the giant's angry strides, managed to yell out, "What on earth possessed you?" he huffed. "Running out like that?"

Dawn said nothing. Draped over the giant's shoulder, she pulled her head up to look into Jorge's cold face. He immediately dropped his gaze, but not before Ulrica could notice the connection. Dawn then looked into her face. Ulrica returned the gaze and walked on with her head high. Marlon finally slowed and stopped. He gently placed Dawn onto her feet, waiting to remove his hands from her shoulders until she was sturdy enough to stand on her own two legs again.

"Listen," he said, pointing a big finger in Dawn's direction. "What you did was foolish, selfish, and irresponsible." He towered over her, like a father reprimanding a child. He took her chin in his hand and looked directly into her eyes, his anger dissolved. "What were you thinking?" he said in a tender voice, his thick black eyebrows pulled together. "We could have lost you to the other side."

"As if you would have cared!" Dawn said coldly, jerking her head away from his hand. "Before any of you try to sweet talk me, I heard you last night and everything you said. I know my soul is of no importance to you. I know that only Josiah matters. I know that you would rather leave me here alone." She was staring into Jorge's now-apologetic face. Dawn's eyes were cold as ice on a windy day, she had no warmth for him. He shrugged and gave a fleeting look to Ulrica before looking down at the leaves on the forest floor.

Marlon began, "Wh . . . wait a second! What are you talking about?"

"Were you not in the room last night when everyone was debating the 'right choices'?" Dawn put her fingers up to sign the quotation marks. "You don't need me to save the world, I will just get in the way. Or don't you remember?" Dawn was now staring coldly into Marlon's confused face. As she looked up into his dark-brown eyes, she realized he didn't know. He had no idea what she was talking about. He turned and searched the others for answers; they each turned their head in shame. Marlon began to put the pieces together. Dawn watched as his face fumed with anger.

"You were having a meeting without the elders?" He turned to face Ulrica, who now faced him, squaring her shoulders. Although Marlon would have had to bend his knees to look her directly in the face, she made no move to back down.

"You take things too lightly, Marlon!" Ulrica spoke with her hands, and her finger was now directly in his face. "Decisions have to be made, and they have to be made fast!" She backed away from Marlon and directed her words to everyone. "Each hour that passes is one that we *lose* and they *gain*. I am sure they know by now where we are and that we have the soul." Dawn was the only person she didn't look at when she spoke. "Make no mistake! They will come, and if we are not ready, God help us. And you know he won't!"

Dawn was confused by her last words, but no one spoke to say otherwise. This confused her more. *I thought God was always there for me* she thought.

"So you keep the elders out of your decision making? Just like old times," Marlon said, shaking his head in disgust.

"We don't have time for your counsel and deliberation. We need to act now!" Ulrica was fiery and her hair began to rise.

"If that's the case, why even come back for me then?" Dawn interrupted.

"Because the baby needs you!" Ulrica snapped. "We have been unable to calm him since you left. And we can't take a crying baby into these woods. We wouldn't make one hundred yards."

"He's crying?" Dawn went from angry to inconsolably worried in a split second. "Why wasn't that the first thing to come out of your mouth?" Dawn took off in the wrong direction, and Marlon reached his arm out and faced her the right way.

Once they arrived back at camp, Josiah was thrust into Dawn's open arms.

"Please." Maribelle was in tears. Silver lines ran down her beautiful face like the arms of a river and spotted the brown blanket Josiah was bundled in. "Make him stop! He's gotten worse and worse!" The moment Dawn held Josiah in her arms he quieted.

"I am so sorry!" Dawn whispered. "That was foolish of me." She began to hum a lullaby and bounced him gently in her arms. He reached his hand up and grabbed his favorite curl and fell asleep instantly. His face was silver-blue and red, a combination of tears and exhaustion.

Dawn looked up at the crowd around her. Everyone was astonished that she had been able to silence him so quickly. These were her friends. Bancroft and Marlon stood side by side, mouths open in astonishment. Maribelle went to Jorge who held her. Jorge had the same sullen face he always wore, but Maribelle's white smile was shining through her tear-painted face. There were neighbors that Dawn only saw once or twice, at training, or walking the opposite direction in the hallway. Everyone was shocked at how fast Josiah stopped crying. The sun shone down on the two as she rocked him and looked up to see the faces. Maribelle left Jorge's side and went to touch Dawn's shoulder; Dawn backed away from her touch. Maribelle stood on her little ballerina toes and looked with her chocolate-brown eyes into Dawn's face. The tears were already beginning to evaporate, and Dawn could see her beauty beginning to shine through again.

"I tried everything, everything!" She pleaded with Dawn, "Please, please forgive me. I . . ."

"Listen," Dawn interrupted, slicing the air with her free hand. "I am not here to be friends with *any* of you." She was addressing the entire village, looking everyone in the face, everyone except Marlon and Bancroft, who were standing in the back. The giant had his arm slung over the lumberjack's shoulders. Everyone watched her intently. "I am only here to get Josiah's soul where it belongs. I am only here for *him*. So please," she said as she straightened her back and raised her chin, demanding continued attention. "I am not here to make false friendships and have small, meaningless conversations. I know how you feel about me now, so let's not pretend. Just show me the way and address me when needed." She took one last look into everyone's shocked faces and noticed a slight smile on Ulrica's lips. "Just don't talk to me."

Dawn went back to her room. With every step, she went deeper into the earth. The dirt and smell paralyzed her thoughts. She just wanted to run, run back to the woods, to the garden, back to Kale. She smiled at the thought of Kale, but as she entered her room and lay next to Josiah on the bed, she realized she wasn't unimportant or insignificant. Josiah needed her; they all needed her. She suddenly felt cold in the earthen room and remarkably lonesome.

Before her adventure last night, one look at Josiah could fill her heart. *He was all I ever needed. All I ever wanted. But now, I just feel empty* she thought. So much was missing. So many details. She realized there was a whole other world out there, an amazingly beautiful world, and once again, she was cooped up inside her brown jail, with no window, no fresh breeze, no Kale.

"Oh, Joey, you would have loved it!" she said, smiling again, looking at him sleeping, wrapped tight in his blanket. "It was so beautiful." She got up from the bed. "The trees were glowing," she said as she walked around the little room. With each step, she seemed to remember a little more of the night before. It warmed her; she felt elated and free. "There were the most beautiful snakes." She chuckled. "I know! I hate snakes!" she exclaimed to the sleeping baby. "But they were beautiful, and then all the petals came down. And it was so amazing. You would have loved it." She sat back on the bed. "It was so beautiful, and then . . ."

"Do you always talk to yourself like this?" Ulrica was standing in Dawn's room, closing the door behind her.

"I thought I was pretty clear on not wanting to talk to anyone," Dawn said stiffly. Her smile had vanished and her sparkling, cool eyes frosted over. Ulrica came in and sat at the foot of the bed. Dawn rolled her eyes and stood up, throwing her hands over her head. "What is it you want now, Ulrica?"

"I have been waiting so long to see if you would ever anger," Ulrica said satisfied.

"What? Are you crazy? Get OUT!" Dawn ordered, pointing toward the door with one hand on her hip. Ulrica didn't move. She just sat on the bed, smiling.

"Fine, then, I'll go." Dawn went for the door. Ulrica stopped her by grabbing her wrist. Dawn pulled back quickly. "Don't touch me."

"Will you just listen? I have come here to talk with you," Ulrica said. "Calm down!"

"Just say what you have to and then please leave," Dawn whispered and took her seat next to Josiah on the bed.

"I've been waiting to see if you would ever become a woman or if you would always remain a scared child."

Dawn looked over to Ulrica. "Oh, so now you are going to tell me you were testing me?"

"Oh, no," Ulrica said snickering. "You were not supposed to hear our conversation. It would have been easier to have you believe you were important." Ulrica looked into Dawn's eyes and smiled.

"I am important." Dawn didn't divert her gaze. Ulrica smiled more. For a second, a feeling of nostalgia swept over Dawn, as though they were old friends reunited.

"Now you passed my test," Ulrica said softly.

Dawn looked at Ulrica. She was so beautiful. Her hair was in two separate braids. As usual, each shoulder bared the weight of one thick braid. A turquoise necklace fell onto her white top, which fit loosely on her firm torso. Ulrica's hands were folded in her lap, and her dark eyes looked peacefully over to Dawn as though she were waiting for her to snap a picture.

"You might not want to eavesdrop in the future," she finally spoke. "No one has been against you. Jorge and I weren't really sure you were ready to go to war. I'm still not sure you are ready," she said as she played with a silver ring she wore on her index finger. She looked down at the ring and turned it a few times over. "But, that's not a bad thing. There are many people here in the camp who aren't ready for war." She looked up from the ring and looked at Dawn. Dawn sat listening intently with one leg propped up on the bed, her fingers were playing with the strings on the bottoms of her brown capris. "Do you think you are ready? What happened in those woods?"

Dawn smiled; her insides warmed as she remembered Kale and his kiss. "Nothing," she said bashfully, quickly changing the subject. "What's the deal with you and Jorge?"

Ulrica directed her attention to her braided leather belt, singling out one turquoise bead and then another and then another. She smiled with one corner of her mouth and then looked back up to Dawn as she rubbed her straight nose with her long fingers.

"You were in the Garden of Eden," Ulrica said, looking directly at Dawn. "The beautiful garden, with the glowing trees, that was the Garden of Eden."

"You just avoided my question." Dawn's eyebrows frowned as she pointed out the obvious. Dawn again focused on her capris, torn between the two mysteries. Dawn asked, "You mean, like, the Garden of Eden from the Bible?"

"Yes, that very garden." Ulrica smiled, relieved that Dawn took the bait.

"Are you sure?" Dawn was once again speechless and confused. "But how, no, wait. Who is Jorge to you?"

Ulrica sulked and placed her busy hands on the edge of the bed. She looked over her shoulder to make sure the door was still shut.

"After I tell you, I don't want to ever have to bring it up again."

Ulrica dropped her head. "Jorge, he, he is my brother."

Dawn's eyes widened and her hands became still in her lap. She sat across from Ulrica, silent and waiting for more.

Ulrica picked up her belt and once again began playing with the stones that dangled at the end; they clinked as she handled them. It was as though she were unable to speak unless her hands were busy.

"He is my twin," she said, not looking up. "We did everything together. He was my very best friend. When we went to war with the other tribe, the chief told me 'no'. No, he wouldn't have a woman go to war. 'Women aren't meant to be warriors.' I told my father, the chief, I would not let Jorge—Rowtag was his name then—leave on his own. My father forbade me to accompany Rowtag, and then he hugged me and kissed me and told me he loved me. 'Watch over your brother' were his last words. He knew I was going to go." Ulrica looked up and into the clay wall. "I did everything with my brother. We fought together, we died together, we rose together." She lowered her head again.

"When we got here to the spirit world, we found our ancestors. Back then they weren't hard to find. Nobody hid underground in fear like today, like cowards. Once we were settled in our new home, they told us of war and of good spirits and bad. They told us there was one spirit man who controlled the others, and that he lived in the clouds."

God? Dawn thought.

"We were told he desperately wanted our souls, he needed our souls. So we entered battle after battle, fighting for freedom, fighting for everyone else. We went to trainings to learn how to use all of our souls. The powers I have were not given to me. I just had to unlock the wolf inside me. My brother was much, much more dangerous.

"It wasn't long before we entered a battle we could not win. And we got separated. His soul was taken to the clouds where they kept him alive and gave him a new shell. But I swear," Ulrica looked up into Dawn's watchful gaze, "he's not my brother." Two silver tears streamed down Ulrica's high cheeks.

Dawn reached over and took Ulrica's slender hand into her own. *How could these hands ever hurt anyone?* she thought.

"Thank you," Dawn whispered. "So, I was in the Garden of Eden?"

Ulrica looked up and smiled, thankful for yet another change in conversation. "Yes." She squeezed Dawn's hand before letting it go. "The wonderful garden."

"You know I'm hungry to know more, right?" Dawn looked over to the sleeping babe and fixed his blanket.

"You know that it's not necessary to cover him, right?" Ulrica pointed out.

"Yeah, I pretty much figured that," Dawn said, still fiddling with the blanket. "Habit, I suppose."

"God thought that he could contain the human, *Manitou,* spirit, in that garden. He thought if he took them away from everything that they would remain pure. So he sat two souls in a garden and gave them everything they wanted. He gave them anything and told them, 'You cannot eat from that tree, that tree is forbidden.' You know the story." Ulrica was speaking with her hands. "But God misled that couple by calling it the tree of knowledge. The tree really had no power. It was just there for temptation. There can be no sin without temptation. He wanted to see if his new creation would be able to withstand the temptation, even if it was only a mere apple. After a short while, human nature kicked in. Although they had everything, they still wanted more."

"So the Devil, the snake, had nothing to do with the fall."

"Eve never spoke with the snake. Have you ever spoken with an animal and had it talk back? The snake, however, was her favorite animal, and it was there when they took the first bite, *together.*

"Curiosity is a powerful trait, and we would be robots without it. When they finally broke the rule, God was angry with them and the angels cried. Or so they say. I honestly can't see any of them showing an emotion other than hate." Dawn sat with her eyes wide and mouth open. "Oh, yeah! By the way, the truth can be sometimes hard to swallow, but you asked for it!" Ulrica smiled, wagging her index finger in Dawn's direction.

"So, after breaking the rules, Adam and Eve were sent to live in the world. Thrown in and confused. That was their punishment for disobeying, if you can remember the scriptures. And to God's amazement, they loved it! They loved meeting other souls and having children and being able to love one another. The adventures they were able to have!

"Dawn, human souls, well, any soul for that matter, is not meant to be locked, whether in a cell, home, or even in a beautiful garden. We are meant to be free. I fight for freedom. I no longer fight for him or her, I fight for freedom for me and for those I love."

"Her?" Dawn cocked her head to the side.

Ulrica smiled like never before. "Are you a woman or a babe?"

"I'm definitely feeling like a babe right now," Dawn replied as Ulrica stood and began to head for the door. "Will you tell me more?"

"Yes, you need to know what's at stake and what you are getting your soul into. Not that you aren't going to make the journey anyway."

With those last words, Ulrica walked out of the room, nearly catching her skirt in the door.

Dawn stared at the door for a moment, sitting at the edge of her bed, paralyzed. Her mind was flooded with Ulrica's words. *Did I really just have that conversation? Am I dreaming? What powders has Ulrica blown into the room this time? No, I'm not dreaming. But is it all true?* Dawn laid her head on her pillow and allowed her mind to race as she watched Josiah sleep.

Chapter 11

Love Thy Enemy

"You have to guard yourself. Stop trying to attack me!" Marlon made a loud teacher. "You have to remember that you are carrying Joey. We will fight for you," he cringed, "if need be. You are not a fighter; you are the defender. Now, hold that pillow as if it were Joey," Marlon barked.

The training grounds were alive today. The sun shone brightly, and one could almost see the energy. Ulrica looked on from her spot in the grass, sitting with her legs crossed and juggling her daggers, smiling the way she does when she is thoroughly entertained. Bancroft was sparring with the twins, Benjamin and Samuel. They towered over him, like shadows in the late-summer hours. Each held one long, red oak staff with rounded ends. Bancroft wielded a short, thick staff. He jumped, dodged, and goaded them on.

"Ha, ha. You gonna have to try harder than that, boys!" he hooted as he jumped over Benjamin's swing and popped him on the head with his own staff.

"We just don't wanna hurt you, old man!" Samuel laughed as he lunged forward, hitting Bancroft with a solid blow to the chest. The blow sent Bancroft flying and falling in front of Ulrica, who in turn, lost track of her daggers, allowing them to fall on either side of her.

"Quit playing around, honey." She planted a kiss on his forehead, took his staff and gracefully rose to spar with the twins, leaving him alone in the shade. He took off his armor and rubbed his bare belly as he laid down in the shade.

"That's better, Dawn. You go take a break now and I will be back to spar some more with you. I have to go check on the others."

Marlon dismissed Dawn, hugging her before he went about his way.

Dawn looked around. It was a beautiful sight to see so many people out on a sunny day. She spotted Bancroft lying in the shade and took a seat next to him in the grass. For a moment she sat in silence, taking in her surroundings. People were busy sparing, teaching, or sharpening their skills or weapons. Ulrica was bracing herself on her husband's small staff as she mediated a fight between the twin towers, Samuel and Benjamin, and a black man in a purple suit with a cane that Dawn had never seen before. Before sparring, the man with the suit tipped his purple hat to the men in overalls. Dawn was eager to see this fight. The twins had arms like rockets. Their white T-shirts were tight around them and their overalls loose. *Click, clack, click, swoosh, click.* They had begun their match. It hardly seemed fair. One skinny man in a suit versus two men who were almost as tall and wide as Marlon. To Dawn's surprise, the man in the suit was graceful; he danced about the men with the elegance of a professional fencer.

"Urg," came a noise from beside her. Bancroft was trying to sit up. Shirtless, his round, white belly wasn't floppy, but one firm mass. When he saw that Dawn was looking at it, he smacked it a couple of times. "Ha, ha. You wanna feel how rock hard this is?"

"Um," Dawn started laughing, "no thanks."

As she looked away to avoid taking in anymore of Bancroft's belly, she spotted a couple giggling under an oak tree. The man was holding his skinny, long-legged woman in his thick arms. Dawn was sure he was singing his blonde love a sweet ballad, but she could only imagine the tune. She continued to stare at them. How perfectly content they seemed, lying in each other's arms. How good it must feel to be held. She breathed an envious sigh and thought of Kale, how his hands seemed to mesh perfectly in hers, how comfortable she was in his embrace.

"Oh," Bancroft broke in, putting his shirt back on. "Sheila and Ogre. Those two love birds." Bancroft was now sitting up smiling.

"If anyone ever loved anyone, it's those two. Some people are lucky when they come into this realm," he said as he slipped his hairless arm into one of his blue suspenders. "They have their family waiting for them, greeting them, bringing them here or there or wherever home is."

"They don't talk," Dawn noticed.

"They don't need to. They are soul mates." He reached behind himself for his flannel shirt; his fingers fumbled for his pipe. "When Ogre passed, he waited five years in the same spot. He never moved; he just waited." Bancroft told the story as though it were a well-known fable. He paused as he lit his pipe. "He sat on a rock over by the cliffs," he puffed, "over by where we found you." He puffed again. "He was like a gargoyle on that cliff. He waited for her, unable to move without her. It was as though he had died. We were afraid he would turn to a sliver with no interaction. But he didn't.

"Then one day, before sunset, she came to the realm." He was no longer looking at the couple; he had propped himself on his elbow and watched as his smoke rose through the shade. "She knew where he was and he knew she was coming. She came like an angel. She floated to the big teddy bear and held him. They sat there for three months, on the edge of that cliff, just holding each other. Never speaking, never moving. Then one day she got up and held out her hand." Bancroft exhaled, "That was the first time he had moved in *five* years."

"So that's what love is?" Dawn still had her eyes on the blissful couple.

"I'm watching you."

Dawn smiled and looked about her.

"No, love is how they got here. That was just patience and faith in love."

"What happened?" She now turned her direction to Bancroft, intrigued.

"They were two souls who loved each other in the face of adversity. Her father was some rich, important man, and her brother was his crazy successor. He wasn't gonna have Ogre's blood in the family." Bancroft tapped his pipe. "One day they were caught trying to run away together. The brother had them both beaten. He made Ogre watch as his men beat his sister, and then made Sheila watch as they killed him."

"Oh, my God, that's awful." Dawn covered her mouth with her hand.

"It was an awful thing that happened. But look at them now. You would never know." Bancroft reached out to Dawn with his free hand. Her hand seemed frail in his thick hand. He gently squeezed it and looked in her aqua- blue eyes, the color they got whenever she was emotional. "Dawn, listen. We have all had our share of pain. We were all human. You always have to remember that you *cannot* forget the past, but you *must* keep moving forward."

"He looks like such a teddy bear," Dawn said as she peered over again at the two soul mates. "Why the name Ogre?"

"If you ever see him fight, you will understand." Bancroft got up and dusted off his jeans. "Well, come on, little love, let's work on your offense."

"Finally!" Dawn said happily, jumping up to train. "I thought you'd never ask!"

That night the underground fortress was quiet. Dawn sat in her plain room, cradling Josiah in her arm. She spent her time staring into the walls. The roots looked like veins running up and down the brown earth. The candle on the nightstand shone bright, never flickering, never going out. She had never been in the room without light. She had never blown the candle out. There she sat, after a long day's work and training, wanting more. She desperately wanted to see the night sky again, among other things.

She got up and left her room, walking with Josiah bundled and silent, through the mud halls. It felt as though the tunnel just got longer and narrower, looking like a throat closing up to an allergy. She was being swallowed by the earth.

She rapped on the wooden door belonging to Maribelle and Jorge. "I'm only going out for some fresh air," Dawn told Maribelle, handing over Josiah, making sure to support his head as he exchanged arms. She pulled down his blanket and planted a delicate kiss on his forehead. "Be back soon."

"Not too far now." Maribelle wagged her short finger at Dawn. "I don't think I can handle a repeat of last time."

"No, no, I am just not used to being underground," explained Dawn, wiping the sweat beads from her forehead, leaving a shiny smear behind.

"I used to get claustrophobic too," Maribelle sympathized. "Eventually you get used to it. Do you have your daggers?"

Dawn patted her hips, "Yes, I'm armed."

"Okay, and have you told anyone else." Maribelle looked up at Dawn, painfully reminding Dawn of her mother.

Dawn became inpatient standing in the doorway. Tears were stinging her eyes, but she wasn't sad. "No, I'm just go . . ."

"Oh, I know where you *said* you were going. I also know where you *will* be." Maribelle was smiling now as she leaned on the door frame. "I know he won't hurt you, even though he's a Gid . . ."

"Whoa, shhhhh." Dawn grabbed Maribelle by her shoulders and pushed her through the doorway, quickly closing the door behind them. Once inside, she realized this was the first time she had ever been in anyone's room. It differed greatly from hers. There was a desk in the corner with vials and herbs resting on top. A bigger bed than hers was in the middle of the room, and a shelf with trinkets on it was above the bed. There was a small carpet on the floor that had been woven from straw. Bundles of wildflowers hung upside down from the ceiling, drying.

"Who else knows?" Dawn said hurriedly, her hand still on the door. She pushed down on the handle, ready to leave.

"Just me," Maribelle said smiling, rocking the sleeping babe in her arms, pressed fully upon her big bosom. Her wide hips swayed to a music that wasn't playing; her little feet danced to and fro. "You think Ulrica is the only one who has tricks around here?"

"Ummm." Dawn stared dumbfounded and speechless.

"I see things that could be, would be, or should be."

"You see . . . ?"

"He's waiting, you know. He's been waiting for a few days now." Dawn opened her mouth to speak. "Well, go on. You don't have too long." Maribelle began to usher Dawn out of the room with her free hand. "I'll cover for you."

Dawn exited into the common area that she was growing accustomed to. She inhaled deeply, taking in the fresh scents of the forest, which was foreboding and dark. The moon wasn't shining, and little light came from the thousands of stars above her. She peered into the forest; it was darker than she remembered. She walked up to the mighty oak tree that usually provided her shade and sat on the flat rock beneath it.

"What now?" She sat, defeated, with one arm supporting her pouting head and the other lying limp at her side. "I'm so stupid," she whispered as she put her head in her hands.

Dawn heard a twig break behind her. She snapped her head around and stared into darkness.

"Who's there?" she called out, reaching her hands down to her belt. "Kale, is that you?"

From behind the tree his head popped out; his long, thin dreadlocks were hanging freely. "Are you alone?" he whispered.

"Yes. I wanted to come find you, but it, it's just too dark. I got scared. I'm sorry."

"You are right to be scared, and don't apologize. You did everything right." He reached his hand out from behind the tree. "Come with me. I can't be seen."

Dawn reached out and held his hand. Behind the tree he greeted her with a bone-melting kiss; she became putty in his arms. He led her into the forest, holding her hand firmly in his as they walked slowly and silently into the blackness. They walked up to an ancient elm tree. Its trunk was so wide it would have easily taken six people to encircle it. There were knobs all over the trunk, and its branches looked thick and sturdy. It was as though the tree were begging to be climbed.

"Can you climb this?" Kale motioned to the tree that was so enormous the top could not be seen from the base.

Dawn smiled, as she was reminded of her younger years when she would spend entire afternoons perched in the tree in her backyard, watching the neighborhood children playing at the park behind her house. She frowned when she remembered what it was that made her climb the tree in the first place. Kale looked into her face, waiting for an answer.

"Come here. I will give you a boost." There was a rustle in the bushes and Kale spun around. "We need to get up this tree." Turning back to Dawn with his hands interlocked and open, ready for her foot, he panicked to see she had disappeared.

"Dawn," he whispered. "Dawn." His eyes were wide with fear, and his dreadlocks swayed to and fro. Dawn giggled and whistled from a branch above his head. "Impressive," Kale stated before he scaled the tree himself. As Kale came up behind her, Dawn went higher into the tree, grabbing the braches like handles to a ladder. They finally settled near the top of the tree on a solid, smooth branch. Dawn looked out into the forest and marveled at how much she could see from up there. The base gave itself away with a billowing smoke cloud, and in the opposite direction, she spotted the glow of The Garden. She closed her eyes and took in the salty air of the ocean.

Dawn was leaning against Kale, who had his back against the

tree trunk. He held her as though they were riding a horse, straddling the branch. "You owe me a story." She smiled and held his arms tighter around her waist.

"I do."

"Are you really a Gidly?"

"Yes, of course." His chest puffed with pride.

"But I don't understand. If you're evil, why . . ."

"Who said anything about evil?"

"Bancroft, Marlon, the others." Dawn shrugged her shoulders in confusion.

Kale chuckled. "What else do *they* tell you, Dawn?" Dawn could tell he was smiling by the way his words eased out. "Do you ever question what you are told?"

"I don't know." Dawn felt like a child again, hiding in the tree, ignorant and naïve. "Why are you laughing at me?"

"I'm not. Do you think I am evil?"

"No."

"You know," he pulled her hair back over her shoulder and began running his fingers through it. "When you die, the knowledge you had in life follows you in death."

"Meaning?" She closed her eyes. It felt good to have his fingers in her hair.

"Meaning, let's say you believe that God is in Heaven and the Devil is in Hell. When you die, you will still believe that, even though what you know might be wrong.

"Unfortunately, when we die, we do not become all knowing. No one brings us the book of life's mysteries solved. In truth, there is much more to be learned in death than there is in life."

"Well . . ." Dawn began.

"Shhh, it's my turn, remember?" he whispered in her ear. "Which way is Heaven?" Dawn pointed her index finger up. "And Hell is?" She pointed her finger down. "And tell me, Hell is . . ." He paused, holding her hair in his hands.

"Hot, sulfur and ash, brim . . ."

"Hell is where I live," he interrupted. "Marlon and Bancroft and the others, they believe what they have been told." He began playing with her hair again. "Hell is hot and the Devil has horns. But I assure you that she doesn't. Just ask Ulrica. She has seen her."

"Her?" Dawn's pursed her lips, and her eyes stared into the darkness below her.

"If you wanted to rule a country or land, how would you go about it?"

Dawn wasn't sure; her mind was still stuck on the pervious sentence. She redirected her gaze to the sky. She watched as the millions of stars twinkled at her, one for each of her questions, and they all laughed at her ignorance. *You guys are always mocking me!* she thought. *Do I know anything? Is he telling me the truth?*

"You would spread propaganda," Kale answered, playing the student and the teacher.

"God is not a dictator." Dawn blinked fast and shook her head as though the words Kale uttered could simply fall back out of her ears, if she could only find enough strength to push them out. "This is blasphemous." She was angry and moved her torso away from his. "I still have a chance to get into heaven. You're, you're, you're just like the Devil in the desert with Jesus. You're testing me. Well, I won't fall for it!" Dawn raised her voice and pointed her finger into the face of darkness. "You're . . ." She took a breath and whispered, "You're evil."

Twisting the hair on her head into a bun, Kale whispered, "Really, do I feel evil?"

"No, but . . ." Dawn remembered the words Maribelle said earlier. Kale snapped a twig of the branch, smoothed it out with his nails, and stuck it into her hair to hold the bun in place. He took her frantic hands in his and pulled her body back until he held her firmly against his chest again.

"Shhhhh, we don't have much more time," he said as he held

her hands on her stomach. "Here's my story. A long, long time ago," Kale began, "there was a God. He ruled over earth and all its sister realms. You know them as Heaven and Hell and this realm we are in now.

"Well, God had followers. Angels. Many of them. But one in particular he favored most. Lucifer. She was beautiful, and he loved her more than the others."

"Stop, wait." Dawn swallowed hard. "Lucifer is a man."

"No, Lucifer, also known as the Devil, also known as Venus. We call her Lucy for short. Now, no more interruptions, please. Time is short." He squeezed her tighter around the waist. "You *need* to know this."

"Okay," Dawn whispered. She wanted to panic, but something about Kale kept her grounded. There was something tremendously fascinating about this person: his voice, his touch, his spirit.

"As I was saying, God fell in love. Lucifer returned that love. One day they decided to each give a part of their souls, their essence, to form a being that would be theirs and theirs alone. They both loved this soul, but the only way this soul could grow and mature would be to place it into a human body. It had to be given birth to. So along came Mary."

Dawn sat up straight and swung her legs around the branch with the ease of a gymnast. She searched Kale's face for any signs of a joke or hoax. His dark eyes sparkled, reflecting the white-hot stars from above. His full lips were not smiling.

"This is crazy," Dawn said defiantly. "I can't . . ." Kale put his hand up to cover Dawn's mouth.

"The story is almost over. And you have to go very soon, so please, just listen." He pleaded again and then held her hands as their knees pressed against one another's. "God and Lucy fought while the soul was on earth. Lucy felt the child should be rich and know his worth, while God felt he should live humbly. You know, build character." He pulled Dawn closer; she was no longer sitting on the tree branch but securely in his lap. She laid her head on his chest and let him stroke her back as she continued to listen in disbelief.

"Lucy also wanted more power. She felt that if God really loved her, he would make her his equal. She wanted to sit on a throne as high as his."

"Blasphemy," Dawn whispered. Her body was like the beach on a calm day, and her mind was like the water hitting the shore. The questions resembled the surf. One after the other breached the sand. Before one could be fully answered, another wave came in just as strong.

"That's what God said. Eventually, God had enough. He loved her very much but just couldn't give up the power. He figured his love should have been enough. After all, this was all his. It wasn't long until their relationship fell apart and went sour. God had Lucifer and her followers kicked out of Heaven, and he sent them to Hell, the smallest of the realms. He gave Hell to Lucy as her own realm, to rule as she saw fit. Soon the power began to shift. A new way of thinking and belief came about on earth. A god is only as strong as his worshipers. And that's when the long and never-ending war for power began."

There was a heavy rustling in the woods not far behind them. "Dawn, we have to go now! Climb down. Hurry!" When they reached the base of the tree, Kale grabbed Dawn's hand and whispered as they ran, "You have to remember, there is good and evil in all of us."

They had reached the base much faster than Dawn had expected. *Why is it the trip back always seems faster than the trip there?* she thought. Dawn lowered her head. She knew what was to come now: another goodbye, another kiss that would leave her yearning until the next time.

"I need you to know that I will be watching. I lo . . ." Kale interrupted himself and kissed her long and deep under the massive oak tree by the stone. He held her head in his hands, and she caressed his neck. "Ask Ulrica. She knows everything. You can't ever leave by yourself again." There was more rustling in the woods behind them. Kale turned his head and his dreadlocks spun in unison. He turned back to Dawn with a frightened look in his dark eyes. They shared another full kiss and he fled, sprinting toward the rustling.

As Kale disappeared into the darkness, Dawn ran in the opposite direction, hurriedly tapped a sequence on the tree she knew to be the door, and entered safely. Her mind trailed as she walked down the brown halls.

"Did you get good air?" Maribelle said to the shell-shocked Dawn who stood outside her door. "Ooo, I like what you did with your hair." Dawn nonchalantly touched her head and felt the bun. Maribelle carefully handed her Josiah. "I don't think anyone has even missed you. They are still in a meeting. Apparently, something important came up."

On the way back to her room, a woman with long red hair went flying past her. She stopped in the hall only a few feet from Dawn and turned around. The woman was drenched in metallic-blue soul, making her hard to recognize. It was her scarlet-red hair that revealed her identity. There were only two people in Dawn's entire existence that had hair that shone so violently red, and they were both here in this realm. Shannon and her sister, who was now standing horrified, panicked, and covered with soul in front of Dawn.

"Kelly?" Dawn whispered.

"Where is everyone?" Kelly reached out with her soul-covered hands. "Help me." Dawn hadn't known Kelly well, but she was always envious of the way she took the lead, the way she demanded respect. Kelly now stood before her, broken, and this frightened Dawn, who began slowly and cautiously to back away. Kelly charged Dawn and grabbed her by the shoulders. "HELP!" she screamed. Her grip was firm and her green eyes seemed to shake as they searched Dawn's face for an answer. Dawn, paralyzed with fear, closed her eyes and clutched Josiah, who was silent under his blanket. Kelly violently released her, pushing Dawn hard against the hall wall, leaving someone's soul dripping down her upper arms and eventually taking flight into the space around her. Dawn watched as Kelly began franticly knocking on all the doors. "HELP! PLEASE, SOMEBODY! ANYBODY!"

People began coming out of their rooms. Dawn recognized some of her neighbors from the sparring grounds, but did not really know any of them. Kelly stopped yelling as more and more people filled the hall. Her thin arms hung at her sides; her face was blank and defeated. Her hair seemed to be the only part of her that was alive. Maribelle walked out of her room, her face searching for the cause of all the commotion. Once she spotted Kelly, soaked in soul, she raced to her.

"Kelly!" Maribelle caught the tall, thin woman in her arms as Kelly fell to her knees. "Talk to me, sweetie. What happened?"

"They, they need our help. Shannon! Shannon!" Kelly was now deliriously weeping into Maribelle's bosom as she frantically groped her back, trying to pull Maribelle impossibly closer.

The hallway came alive. Neighbors were whispering and disappearing in different directions; they were coming out of doors with weapons and running huddled, to and fro.

"Was it the Gidlies?" an Asian man asked his wife as they poked their heads out of their door.

Dawn suddenly felt a jolt inside of her. *Not the Gidlies* she thought. For a moment's time she was invisible; everyone was hustling about her with a purpose. Dawn was still against the wall where Kelly had left her, holding Josiah, standing like a statue and watching the chaos unfold. She was lost in contemplation as Shannon's soul evaporated from her arms. She heard nothing and felt nothing; she was mentally and physically numb. A massive hand grabbed her shoulder and pulled her out of her zone. The sounds of the hallway began to rush in: the scuffling and shouting of her neighbors;

the clicking and clacking of metal as weapons were handed out; the thumping and thudding of hurried, heavy feet; the slamming and shutting of doors. The atmosphere was deafening, crushing any thoughts that dared to enter Dawn's brain. But the sound that reigned over the rest, like a mountain's jagged peaks over the valleys beneath it, was that of Kelly. She wailed uncontrollably in the arms of Maribelle, who had given up on trying to soothe her with her own sweet voice. Maribelle held the grown woman in her arms like a baby and rocked her as her own silver-blue streaks streamed down her face. *Kale,* Dawn finally managed to think before she realized Marlon was standing in front of her, his big hands on delicate shoulders.

"Go to Ulrica and Bancroft!" Marlon ordered and then shook her once, making her head bob. Her wandering eyes regained focus. "NOW!" he barked.

Fearful, she began walking toward Bancroft's room.

"People! Get ready!" Marlon's voice boomed through the hall, demanding attention. "IT HAS BEGUN!"

Chapter 12

In the Closet

"Ulrica, what's going on?" Dawn asked as she followed Ulrica and Bancroft down a deserted hallway. She wanted to know more about the situation outside, but she was afraid she would give herself away; she did, after all, sneak out to see someone she knew was Gidly. She was afraid if she spoke she would implicate herself. Could she be blamed for the murders? Would Kale be blamed? Would Maribelle tell everyone that she was outside with a Gidly? Would they believe her when she pleaded her innocence? And who was to blame for the rustling noises? What troubled her most of all was that Kale was out there. *I hope he's all right* she thought. She was in dire need of some answers.

"You have everything, correct?" Ulrica questioned Bancroft, ignoring Dawn's question as they took hurried steps down the hall.

"Yes," Bancroft answered. "And you?"

"I have been ready since we got here." Ulrica kept walking, searching left and right. Dawn was trailing behind the two, double stepping to keep up. Josiah was bundled securely in her arms as they sped deeper into the earth. For a moment, Dawn felt like a mole running from a snake; she couldn't see him, but she felt that something sinister was just around the corner. "This is it," Ulrica said, stopping abruptly in front of a narrow wooden door.

"This is what?" Dawn asked as Ulrica rapped a complicated sequence on the wood. *Clink, clank, clank.* The door opened outward, and Ulrica pulled it the rest of the way open. Ulrica pushed Dawn into the room, which was only slightly larger than a closet.

There were no furnishings, no windows, just a candle on the floor and weapons in a corner.

"You two wait here," Bancroft ordered. He kissed Ulrica on her lips, and she took her place next to Dawn. "Someone will be back to get you." He raised his hand to her smooth cheek. "And please, be ready for anything."

"You're always so dramatic," Ulrica answered before kissing him again and pulling the door closed.

An awkward moment passed as the two women stood in the closet. Ulrica put her hand out and motioned for Dawn to take a seat. Dawn sat on the ground, cuddling Josiah in her arms with her back against the wall, facing the door. Ulrica did the same, keeping the candle between them. The light reflected off their faces as they stared at the grain of the wooden door.

"Is there something you need to tell me, Dawn?" Ulrica asked, turning her head to face her. Dawn closed her eyes and gently banged her head against the wall behind her. There was so much she needed to say; there was so much she needed to hear.

"Why won't you just come clean with me?" Dawn said, trying to control her anger and fear. "Just tell me the truth about where I am and what I'm doing here. You can't!" She raised her voice before closing her eyes and pressing the back of her head into the wall with frustration until the twig that held her hair in place snapped. She sighed as she pulled her head forward and her hair tumbled down her back. "You just lie to me and smile, keep me occupied with training and stupid stories. And when I ask you questions that come too close to the truth, you ignore me." Dawn turned her head to look Ulrica in the face. "Why is that?"

"Not too many people know the truth." Ulrica broke her gaze and looked back at the door.

"What truth?" Dawn recklessly threw a hand in the air, almost hitting the candle that sat between them. "You want my entire existence and everything I am. You are training me to fight. *Who* am

I fighting? *What* am I fighting for? Why can't you break even with me?" Dawn felt as though she had a raging bonfire inside of her. Ulrica turned back to Dawn. Her lips quivered and her eyes talked of apology, but no words came out. Dawn looked at her with disgust. "How 'bout I just take the baby and run."

With that, Ulrica's sympathetic disposition changed back to her normal self-assured and slightly cocky demeanor. She smiled and looked back to the door. "We have an army. We would find you."

"Then how about I just find my own army?" Dawn retorted. Ulrica's eyebrows shot up and her smile faded.

"You wouldn't make it out of here," she said plainly, trying to hide her surprise.

"Do you really wanna try me?" Dawn stood and looked down at Ulrica, furious.

Ulrica was shocked to see Dawn physically challenge her. Half stunned and half angered, Ulrica stood to meet Dawn's raging gaze. The two squared up, their eyes sizing each other up, both looking for the other's bluff.

"Do you really think you can handle the truth? You ran away like a child after finding out about Josiah. Jealousy," Ulrica spat. "I don't think you're as strong as you would like to be."

"Of course I ran! I was hurt." Dawn's eyes were wide with emotion; the rage was fading. "I was jealous. I was many things. But I believe in every fiber of my heart that even if I am the lowliest sinner, I still deserve the *truth*. You forget I used to be human." She searched Ulrica for the empathy she so strongly desired.

"A weak one," Ulrica scoffed again, as she crossed her arms and looked away.

Dawn rolled her eyes as she bounced Josiah in her arms. "How can you be so arrogant and selfish? Only you get to know the truth? You just let the rest believe in lies. That's not good enough for me!" Dawn was now yelling and leaning into Ulrica. "Tell me what I am fighting for or *I* will leave! See if you get through the forest without me." Dawn paused, closed her eyes, and took a leap, throwing all caution to the wind. "By the way, Kale says, 'Hi.'"

Ulrica flashed a smile. "It's a welcomed relief to see you have gone from a small child, crying on the floor, to a woman. Almost a warrior." Ulrica praised Dawn as she reached into her skirt pocket. "Fill your lungs with air and blow this dust. Remember, the farther it spreads, the more time we have."

Dawn inhaled and blew the dust. Not a centimeter in the small space remained clear. Ulrica looked about her and laughed, loud and unfiltered.

"Let's sit." Ulrica motioned and the two sat down, leaving trails above them. Dawn watched in awe as the light-blue dust filled her wake. "Not everyone knows what I am about to say because people who know this information don't come to this realm after dying. They go to hell." Ulrica sat cross-legged and motioned with her hands.

"You're a church-goer. So you must know that God is a jealous god. That's why he's the only god with the name God. It has the same effect as a scientist calling himself 'The Scientist.' Who would you rather have solve your problems, Jim or The Scientist?" Dawn envisioned Jim and The Scientist standing next to one another and smiled. "He believed that by calling himself God, the rest were automatically beneath him.

"In the Bible, it says when God created heaven and earth, he wasn't alone. Who do you think those others were? All gods need followers. The more faith you give one god, the stronger he or she becomes, which is why God forbade you to pray to anyone but him. It's the first commandment. That one rule has rendered so many others powerless.

"God and his angels quickly controlled this realm. But every being has a weakness. Love is a killer."

"I know about Lucy," Dawn said quietly. "But why put the soul into a baby?"

Ulrica sat straight and dropped her shoulders. Her black eyebrows arched high; she was visibly taken aback with Dawn's answer.

"Kale has loose lips," Ulrica said, shaking her head. "I would really like to know how much you know." She looked around the light-blue cloud. "However, I don't think time will allow," she sighed. "Jesus was the perfect weapon. A god's soul in a human body. Oh, the damage he could do." She paused and rephrased, now facing off with Dawn who was listening intently while rocking Josiah in her arms. "The damage he did! After his arrival, the Romans and their gods almost completely disappeared. An entire religion and its gods. What are they now? Mere myths, bedtime stories!"

"Why do people think Josiah is the Second Coming?" Dawn looked about hurriedly.

"Because he is." Ulrica replied bluntly. "It worked so well the first time, Dawn. The world, in God's eyes, needs another Messiah. God's been trying for years, but the other remaining gods have caught on to this trick and foil His plan every time."

"But it was just an accident." Dawn became flustered as she remembered her last moment on earth. "We got shot."

"You got shot by a madman—a man who brutally murdered you, your mother, and an infant! Would you say he was *possessed*?" Ulrica asked with wild eyes.

A loud knock at the door startled them both. Dawn took Ulrica's hand in hers.   "Ulrica, who's side are you on?"

"I'm on my side." Ulrica stood tall as she helped Dawn up off the floor. "I fight for no one. I will never again be a pawn in someone else's war."

Chapter 13

The Plan

Benjamin and Samuel, the twin black giants, escorted Dawn and Ulrica from the closet, down the hall, and into a large room. Once in the room, Dawn thanked the men in matching overalls and looked about her. In the front of the room, opposite from where she was standing, were four long tables covered with weapons. There were many more chairs in the room than bodies. All of the chairs were wooden, and all of them faced the tables. Dawn slowly walked closer to the last row and took a seat. She sat alone in the back corner and began to watch the others. For a brief moment, she was reminded of her high school days. *Everything was so simple* she thought. She looked down at Josiah, who was more awake than ever before. His round eyes darted from here to there. In his fat little fist was his favorite curl; in his other was Dawn's pinky finger.

Marlon stood in front of the four tables with Bancroft. Together, they examined the many weapons that littered the front of the room. The pair was deep in discussion. Marlon held a morning star: a large club with scary spikes going through the top end of it. Dawn remembered it from combat practice. She could hardly lift it, but in the hands of the giant, it was a deadly instrument of war, a sheer force to be reckoned with. Bancroft stood, holding his broad ax, fingering the blade with his thumb as he spoke with Marlon. Dawn wasn't sure what they were discussing, but she knew it had nothing to do with the weapons they were holding.

As Dawn continued to look about the room, she counted twenty souls, not including hers or Josiah's. Some were sitting alone; some were standing in circles with their heads huddled together, whispering. Still others were hurriedly scampering up and down the aisle in the middle of the room, busy or nervous. Dawn couldn't tell which. She noticed that whenever she caught the gaze of another by gaze by accident, they either sneered or offered a nervous smile before hurriedly looking in a different direction. She suddenly felt alone in her corner and was thankful when the meeting began.

"Okay, let's get started," Marlon said. He didn't need to yell; his regular voice was enough to permeate the room. "Everyone here or accounted for?" Marlon looked around the room. He made an awkward teacher and looked more like a bull, standing tall and strong. "Okay. As most of you already know, there was an attack only hours ago. We lost two souls." He paused to collect himself. "Mark and Shannon." The congregation gasped in unison. "Our scouts have given us confirmation, Mark's soul has been reaped." A brunette in the second row began to weep. "Shannon's, Shannon is gone." More sobs and wails from the front began to fill the room. "Let's take a couple moments of silence." Marlon bowed his head and took to one knee; Bancroft, who was standing behind him, did the same, as did Samuel and Benjamin, who were standing guard at the door. Ogre held Sheila's head to his broad chest, and others held hands. Dawn now felt like a passerby, a stranger looking in a window at a family during a holiday dinner. Depressed, she lowered her head and allowed the tears to well up in her eyes. But before one could drop, a hand grazed her shoulder. Ulrica had been standing behind her all along. Dawn grew warm and smiled as she kept her head bowed for the moment of silence, thankful not to be alone.

After a moment's time, Marlon stood and wiped a silver tear from his brown skin. "They were good souls." He exhaled, "It is in our best interest to leave this place and join our brothers and sisters in Little Heaven."

"You mean leave here?" Kelly swung her red head up and began to panic. "We are safer here than in the woods!"

"Please, hear me out," Marlon pleaded, his big hands open to the crowd, begging for a handout. He tried to sincerely look everyone in the eyes.

"We will be torn apart in those woods!" another man yelled. He wore a ten-gallon cowboy hat and had spurs on his snakeskin boots. Dawn knew him only as Cowboy Bill. She found it interesting that he looked like a comic book character, yet there wasn't anything funny about him.

"You saw what they did! Why would you make us go out there?" Kelly became hysterical again. Emitt struggled to keep her calm; he forced her to stay seated. He pulled Kelly close and held her slender body to his as he rested his head on hers and stroked her straight hair flat against her back.

"Shhh, Kelly," Dawn heard him whisper.

"We have no choice!" Marlon bellowed. "We stay, we die! You think Gidlies are all we have to worry about? There are reapers and grubs out there, and they *are* taking souls! This is not some little battle anymore. This is a WAR! Them against us!"

"What about the treaty?" a delicate black woman from the back called. Her hair was braided into two cornrows that turned into thick curled braids that rested on her shoulders.

Marlon rolled his eyes, clearly reaching his limit. "Our people were attacked by mid-level demons. The treaty be damned." Marlon shook his head and rubbed his fingers over his black hair that was so short it looked like skin.

The congregation began arguing with one another; words were shot back and forth. Dawn watched as emotions raged and the scene began to unravel. She caught Marlon's eye from the back of the room and held his gaze. She could see the pain, the frustration; she had nothing to offer but a smile. So with sad eyes, she sent Marlon a smile and raised her chin before tucking a strand of hair behind her delicate ear.

Marlon smiled back and bowed his head in thanks to Dawn for

her silent support. He puffed his chest and regained his composure. "People, PEOPLE!" he shouted. Dust fell from the ceiling, reminding Dawn that she was underground and not in a classroom. "Fighting will bring us nowhere."

"If we go as twenty, we will all die," the Asian man from the hallway spoke from the third row. His wife put a proud hand on his shoulder and smiled faintly.

"We won't be going as twenty," Ulrica said as she walked up to the front of the room. Marlon looked at her and nodded, grateful for her support. "We will be traveling in three groups of six."

"Aww, fu . . ." Emitt began as he ran his ringers through his hair, pulling the golden strands away from his face.

"It is the only way," Jorge interrupted. He, too, was now standing and taking his place up front.

"Now please, listen," Jorge began. "The angels are waiting at the mountain top for the soul so as not to further violate any treaties. The higher-level demons have not yet entered this war."

"This is suicide," Kelly shouted. "THIS IS SUICIDE!"

"No, twenty of us going through the forest together is suicide," the black woman from the back rebutted. The hem of her floral dress fell to her ankles as she stood. "We only have to make it to Little Heaven, and then we will be much larger in numbers, right?" she asked, turning her direction to the leaders in front.

"Yeah," Emitt said, rubbing his crooked nose with the back of his hand, "but until then, we are weaker." He held Kelly close to him and kissed her head.

"Thank you, Emitt," Kelly whispered.

"Yes, but in one group, we will be easier to attack. They will single out the baby and it will all be over," the black woman reasoned.

"Charlett is correct." Ulrica supported her, holding out her hand to the woman who was a half a room away.

"I agree with Kelly," another villager said with a Hispanic accent, uncertainty ringing in his voice. "That's small. We will be slaughtered, one after the other!"

Jorge put up his hands. "We *only* have to make it as far as Little Heaven . . . then we will have an army behind us."

"Yes, my friend, but what are the chances of all three groups even reaching Little Heaven? That's almost a half a day's trip," the man with the accent replied.

"Carlos is right. It would take a miracle for all of us to make it safely," Emitt said, no longer holding Kelly, but standing as she nervously clung to his waist.

"It is not of importance if all of us make it," Benjamin said from the back by the door. His twin and the entire room turned to look at him. "It's the baby who *has* to make it! And we all know this. That baby," he said, pointing a strong finger toward Dawn, "that baby's soul is worth all of our souls combined! If I happen to perish while protecting that baby, it will be the greatest honor." Benjamin closed his eyes and smiled. When he opened them, he said, "Maybe it won't come to that. Maybe we will all reach Little Heaven unscratched. That, my friends, is what we should be praying for. Let our prayers be strong and full of faith. Maybe they will be heard. And if not, then may our souls rest in peace . . . wherever they may fall."

"Amen," Bancroft said.

"Amen," the congregation said, as everyone rose together.

"Everyone needs to get ready," Marlon bellowed over the rustling of people getting ready to exit the room. "Take anything that might be of value to you. We leave at sunrise." He then turned to Dawn, who was sitting in the corner at the back of the room, holding Josiah. "Dawn, do you have a minute?"

Dawn nodded. Marlon came to her row and sat in the chair next to her. He took her hand in his and waited to speak until she faced him.

"I care for you deeply. I never got the chance to tell you, after that incident in the woods." Dawn lowered her head. "I would have welcomed your soul here with or without the baby, Dawn." He pulled her chin up to look at her. "You have to believe me."

"I do." She reached her hand to touch Marlon's cheek.

"I won't let anything happen to you. I swear it." Marlon pulled Dawn's face to his and gently kissed her cheek. "Get some rest. We leave when dawn breaks." He cringed after saying the last two words, but Dawn just laughed it off. "You're going to be just fine," he assured her again.

As Marlon rose, he helped Dawn to her feet as well.

"Thank you for everything, Marlon." She reached up and brought his head down to hers and returned his kiss on the cheek.

"This is suicide." Kelly was still sitting in her chair alone, talking to herself. "Suicide," she repeated.

Marlon squeezed Dawn's hand and went over to sit next to Kelly. "Kelly," he whispered.

"Don't tell me my soul is not as important as his," she sobbed angrily into Marlon's chest as his large hand stroked her hair. "I don't want to hear that line. Shannon . . . Shannon was more than that!"

"Shhhhhhh," Marlon rocked her. "I need you to be strong now, Kelly."

"She was my sister!" Kelly screamed as her fists balled up the shoulders of Marlon's black T-shirt. She lifted her face; her green eyes leaked silver blue. "I didn't even get a chance to say goodbye. I love her so much, SO MUCH!" Marlon picked her up and held her seemingly lifeless body in his arms. Her head rested on his shoulders as she continued to mourn the loss of her sibling.

"Come, Dawn. I will take you to your room," Marlon whispered as he led the way with Kelly crying in his arms.

The night was short. Dawn spent it in Ulrica's room, which, not to her surprise, had a counter and cabinets full of herbs. Ulrica's kitchen took up more than half of their quarters. Bancroft sat, smoking his pipe, at a small table that was pushed against the mud wall. He was once again attempting his smoke rings; Dawn smiled at all the different faces he made.

"What's your deal with the smoke rings?" Dawn playfully asked.

"When I was little, there was this wizard in a book I read. He could blow amazing smoke rings." Bancroft sighed as his eyes glossed over with nostalgia. "That was my favorite book."

Ulrica was sifting through powders. She had worked the entire night through, never sitting and never resting; she had just sat and mixed and bagged or bottled. She only spoke to Bancroft and Dawn once, and that was to make sure they had their weapons and their bags packed. Dawn spent the night on their little bed holding Josiah. His eyes were wide with intrigue. He looked about the room and became antsy when Dawn moved too far from the bed.

"It should be morning soon," Bancroft said as he put his feet back into his boots. Lacing them up, he looked about the room.

Dawn was sitting straight up on the bed braiding Josiah's favorite curl. He had finally fallen asleep, and she was able to use two hands again. When she was done braiding, she tied off the end off with some string, from Ulrica's counter. She took a dagger from her belt, and with a quick slice, cut off the thin braid from the root. As she tied off the other end of the braid, she asked, "Ulrica, could you help me with the sling?"

Ulrica said nothing, but wiped her hands on her apron, and for the first time all night, she came from around the counter. Before picking up the sling from the bed, she wrapped her arms around Dawn. Dawn returned the embrace, and for a moment they stood standing in one another's arms.

Ulrica broke away sniffing and turned to get the sling. Dawn turned around and allowed Ulrica to place it on her. She looked over to Bancroft, who smiled as he watched the women.

"That was beautiful," he said.

"Shut up!" Ulrica snapped back playfully. They all laughed together, and when they were done, Ulrica wiped away a tear.

Once Josiah was snug in the sling, Dawn opened his fist and put in the braid, kissing his pudgy fist before placing it securely in the brown blanket. *So you will remember me*, she thought. Before she covered his face, Ulrica and Bancroft both peered in and kissed him gently on his forehead.

There was a knock on the door, and they all solemnly exited the room, one after the other, with Dawn in the middle.

Chapter 14

One Out of Three

Only minutes before departure, the entire village met in the hallway at a cross point in the tunnel that Dawn had never seen before. There were three ways to go: straight, left, or right. All twenty-two souls were huddled together with Marlon in the middle. He looked harder and cold, and it reminded Dawn of the first day she met him.

"Group Bancroft," Marlon pointed out the people as he spoke their names. "Bancroft, Ulrica, Charlett, Benjamin, Samuel, and Andrew. You will be traveling left down this hall until you reach the northern exit." Marlon shifted his weight. "Group Jorge: Jorge, Maribelle, Lily, Jon, Kelly, Cowboy Bill, and Emitt. You all will be exiting through the eastern exit. And my group, me, Dawn, Ogre, Sheila, Elizabeth, and Carlos, we will take this hall down to the western exit." Marlon stood tall as he commanded over his groups. "Remember to keep the decoys in the middle. Protect her or it won't look real." As he spoke, Ulrica tied Josiah closer to Dawn's chest, which was a completely unnecessary action. Josiah's sling was as tight as it could be, and Dawn had full control of both hands. Dawn knew this and so did Ulrica, and yet she continued to silently check the straps. When she was done, she handed Dawn her satchel and her weapons, and the two held hands for a moment.

"You take care of yourself," Ulrica whispered. "I will see you soon."

Maribelle was helping tie a sack of dirt around one of the decoys, a slender Asian woman about the same height and stature as Dawn. "Lily, keep the poncho over your head at all times." Maribelle pulled up the woman's hood, hiding her black, shiny braid. She then grabbed her delicate, porcelain hands and pushed them into the sling. "And hold this sack of dirt *real* tight. Jorge and I will be in front of you; your husband will be closely behind you." Kelly put her hand on Lily's shoulder.

"I'm going to be right here."

"I'm so scared," Lily whispered as she looked over to her husband. Her big, black, almond eyes were drowning in silver tears. Before a tear could fall, her husband grabbed her face in his small hands and kissed her passionately.

As they stood in their lovers' embrace, Samuel tied another sack of dirt to Charlett.

"Listen here, now," he said with a polite Southern drawl. "I don't want nothin' happening to you." Charlett nodded. "You stay under this hood. Tie your hair back. Nothing can give you away." Charlett grabbed her wild curly hair and tied it to the back of her head.

"Now cover that up afro puff!" Benjamin laughed. "I got your back, sister." Charlett smiled nervously and turned back to Samuel, who gently kissed her lips and pulled her hood over her head. He placed a satchel on her shoulders.

"Your daggers?" Samuel asked as he held her hands.

"I have them in my belt," Charlett whispered.

Charlett, Lily, and Dawn stood next to each other.

"They look identical," Cowboy Bill said as he stood and looked at the three women in the brown ponchos. "Let's just pray that dem hoods stay on."

"Do not let anyone see your face." Ulrica wagged her finger. "You all just keep your faces down and no one will know who you are. You will be safe as long as your cover doesn't get blown. Remember, there are eyes everywhere." Ulrica was in front of the three, repositioning Charlett's bag and pulling Lily's hood down more. "We will see each other soon."

The last of the hugs and goodbyes commenced.

"It is time." Marlon had his back to the crowd. No one took offense; they all knew his heart was breaking. "Dawn, get behind me."

The congregation split, and the chatter died down as each group went its separate way. It would be the last time many of them would see Middle Haven.

After what seemed like an eternity to Dawn, her group finally reached the end of the hallway. Marlon rapped the sequence on the northernmost wall of Middle Haven. Before opening the door, he looked back to his group of seven and inhaled deeply.

"Weapons up," he commanded. "Dawn, you stay behind me, always." Dawn tugged at his shirt and Marlon smiled. "Very good. Let's go."

He opened the door and they walked out into darkness. Dawn wanted to look around but was well aware of the rules. Immediately, the musky smell of old water flooded her senses. The ground was rock hard and black. There was a sound like cannons rumbling in the distance. *Great, another cave,* she thought.

They walked straight through a rocky chamber for over an hour. No one made a sound. The damp air seemed to stick to her shell, her hair, and her clothes. She felt heavy and imprisoned. She couldn't feel the tips of her fingers anymore; they had become numb from having to hold on to Marlon's shirt. Dawn and Marlon were no longer two separate people walking through a black cave; her footsteps became one with his. If she had not known there were more people in the group, she would not have believed it. They were all so quiet. The only sound she heard was the sound of falling water thundering against rocks. The sound became louder and more deafening with each step.

Little by little, more of the cave floor became visible. Light was coming from up ahead, a sheer, pale light. It made the rocks on the wet ground glow. Every now and then she would spot a shell's glimmer as she passed by.

Josiah was awake under the blanket. She could barely make out his head in the dim light, yet she knew he was looking up into her face. She could feel it. *Such a good baby.*

Her eyes adjusted to the ever-growing light with pleasure. Finally, she was able to see which stones not to step on. She could make out the swing of the heel of Marlon's enormous black boots and her baby's glistening eyes staring back at her. They were picking up the pace. The cave was so loud that even if she were to shout, she wasn't sure anyone would hear her. The thundering from before was now a deafening, earthshaking growl.

Marlon stopped abruptly. Dawn didn't need to look to know that they were standing in front of a large waterfall. Cool mist sprayed onto Dawn's face. She closed her eyes and let the water wash onto her skin, forming little beads that began to roll off of her cheeks and down her neckline, soaking her clothes underneath. Marlon signaled something that was out of Dawn's sight. For the first time, she saw the feet of her company as they scampered past her. Ogre's heavy boots stepped past, and then came Sheila's dainty green slippers, Elizabeth's brown loafers, Carlos's white sneakers, and lastly, Ferguson's alligator boots and cane.

When only Marlon and Dawn where left, his massive hand pulled her head up by the chin to look at him. He was soaked; water was running down his body as if it were raining. He stood for a second, his tan skin majestically silhouetted against the white and blue raging waters that glowed as the sun shone from the other side. He looked like a statue as he stood in front of her. He looked over to his left toward a gap in the cave wall and the tumbling waters and directed her with one large hand. Dawn lowered her head and put her hand on the outer wall of the cave. The wet stone felt cold and refreshing. Marlon's hand securely grabbed her waist, and it was comforting to know he was directly behind her. He pushed her toward a ledge, and she kept her right hand against the wall.

"Watch your footing," he whispered in her ear before gently

pushing her out onto the ledge.

The sun was so bright Dawn had to squint to see her feet. The wind from the falling water rushed up and grabbed her hood, threatening to expose her face. She was quick to take her free hand and hold it down. When the world finally did come into focus, she became weak at the knees. From under the hood she could see a sparkling-blue lagoon far below her. Jagged rocks begged her to lose her footing; they were grey and hungry and angry. She leaned into the cool wall and rested her body against it to regain her composure. She finally looked into Josiah's bubbling face and began to take small, controlled steps on the ledge. She didn't need to see the whole picture to know there was no room for error.

She kept moving forward with Marlon's hand on her waist, step after step until the thunderous roar of the waterfall was once again just a grumbling in the distance. She found herself breathing, and she wondered how long she had been holding her breath. She quickly looked at Josiah's sleeping face and was comforted. *How is he sleeping?* she thought in disbelief.

She could hear the footsteps of the others as they walked along the ledge, which was sloping downward and, thankfully, getting much wider. Dawn noticed that the rocks from the ledge were getting fewer and that the grass was getting thicker and longer. It was only a matter of minutes before they were walking in waist-high green grass. The blades were thicker than Dawn's fingers, and she was letting them tickle her free hand as she held on to Marlon's shirt with the other. The grass seemed to offer protection. Dawn wanted so badly to lie in it and forget the world. *I could hide here.*

Sometimes she could see the shadows of the others in the green grass blades, and other times the sun shone so brightly that the blades seemed to cut her eyes like razors. Sometimes she would get lost in her daydreams and have to force herself back to reality. She would dream that all of this was just an elaborate nightmare, that she would wake in her bed to the cries of a hungry Josiah. She would dream of her mother's laugh, but she would always be brought back when she remembered how the dream had ended.

Soon the grass began to grow shorter, and briefly after that, the grass disappeared altogether and gave way to the barren forest floor. Large red and brown maple leaves littered the ground. They were soft with dew, allowing the group's footsteps to be silent upon them. The group itself was noiseless, and they bunched closer together now as they walked through the forest. There were many times they all stopped. Dawn hated not being able to look around and see for herself. Despite her feelings and growing curiosity, she obediently kept her head down.

As they walked deeper into the forest, Dawn began to grow uneasy. *Where is Kale?* she thought to herself. They stopped again. Marlon took two steps to the right, allowing the sun to warm her legs. The forest had abruptly ended before them and had opened into a small field.

Flashbacks ran through Dawn's mind. She saw her mother lying lifeless; she saw herself running helplessly through a forest; she remembered the way it felt to be stuck in the mud. Mostly, she remembered staring down the barrels of a shotgun, at the end of which stood a wild-eyed man. She heard the clang of two gunshots. Dawn panicked and yanked on Marlon's shirt, pulling him backward. Her body trembled, but at the same time, she couldn't get her legs to move. Marlon got on one knee and looked under her hood. His black eyes searched her face for an answer to her sudden panic. Tears flooded her eyes and streamed down her face, falling onto the leaves on the forest floor, splattering the crimson leaves with silver drops, like paint on a hardwood floor. Dawn shook her head left and right. Her full lips trembled, and she mouthed the words "Please, no. Please, no." Marlon looked into her eyes and grabbed her hand, interlocking them at the wrist. He pulled her close so that their elbows kissed. Without warning, all seven of them sprinted into the clearing. They were halfway through when a scream from the east stopped them in their tracks.

"*Eiiiiiiiiiiiiiiiiiiiiiiiiiiiiiiiiiiiiiiiiiiiiiiiii!*"

"Maribelle!" Marlon whispered. "Run," he whispered again as he grabbed Dawn by the elbow and took off sprinting. Dawn was holding her hood fast to her head, not sure if her feet 'were even touching the ground. With her other hand she held onto Josiah, who was looking at her as though he knew what was going on. He was eerily awake and silent, aware of the danger.

Marlon reached the forest wall before the rest and turned around to catch Dawn, who was behind him, blindly flying in. She wanted to continue running, but Marlon lifted her off the ground to stop her. Ogre and Sheila were next to make it to the edge of the forest, hand in hand. Carlos and Ferguson came in after them. Elizabeth was last, the denim from her blue jean jacket made her stick out in the green grass of the field.

"How did she get so far behind?" Marlon whispered.

"*Caaaaaaaaaaaaaaaaaaaw!*" Dawn had to fight every muscle in her body not to look up.

"What was that?" she whispered under her breath.

"ELIZABETH, RUN!" Carlos yelled.

"CAAAAAAAAAAAW!" Dawn reached for Marlon with her free hand. She was blindly grabbing at him to get away from the bone-splitting sound. "CAAAAAAAAAAAW!" Terror gripped Dawn, and she clawed her way up Marlon's torso until he was carrying her in his arms.

"What is that?" she spoke out loud, panicked.

"A hell bat," Ferguson whispered. "She's not gonna make it."

"No! Nooooo!" Carlos began to leave the shelter of the forest, but Ferguson held him back. "NOOOOOOOOOOOO! LET ME GO! LET ME GO! ELIZABETH!" Ferguson was twice the size of Carlos and still had trouble holding him back.

"*CAAAAAAAAAAAAAAAAAAAAAAAAAAAAAAAAAAAW.*" Dawn could fight it no longer. She looked up from under the hood to see the hell bat. Its body was as big as a horse. Its bat-like wings were fully stretched, and its dark-red eyes had zeroed in on its prey. Its body dipped as it swooped its leathery black wings, casting a dark, sinewy shadow over Elizabeth, blowing the grass around her as it came down and grabbed her screaming body into its black claws. Dawn threw her hood back over her head, frozen in disbelief as to what she had just witnessed.

"NOOOOOOOOOOOOOOOOOOOOOOO!" Carlos yelled as he fell to his knees sobbing.

"Get up!" Ferguson pulled him by his arm. "Damn it, Carlos, get your ass up!"

Carlos stayed on his knees, head cupped in his hands, distraught from watching the fate of his friend. Ferguson signaled to Ogre, and they both grabbed him under the arms and quickly went deeper into the forest.

"Aiiiiiiiiiiiiiiiiiiiiiiiiiiiiii!" There was another blood-curdling scream. Marlon stopped.

"No, no," he whispered, as he and the others faced west, looking into the woods as though they could see the action. "Not Ulrica."

Dawn's head shot up.

"Caaaw, caw." A raven from a nearby branch took flight. Sheila grabbed the back of Dawn's head and fiercely pushed it down onto Marlon's chest.

"It's too late anyway," Marlon said defeated as he placed Dawn back onto her feet. "We need to run!"

They sprinted through the forest past trees and leaped over bushes. Marlon huffed as he jumped trees, looking back every few seconds to check on his group. Dawn's hood had completely come off, and her hair was flying wildly behind her. Carlos was running on his own again. His face was blank as his body went through the motions. Their faces shimmered metallic as the branches and twigs reached out to cut them like the menacing fingers of a monster. Any limb uncovered suffered the wrath of the forest.

The trees began to thin out, and the group could see further. Skinny alpines began dominating the larger, fuller trees. The forest began to look like pieces of a scattered picket fence. The leaves on the white, thin branches were a vivid rusty red. The forest floor looked as though it were bleeding, so many leaves had fallen. Marlon's pace slowed, and eventually the group came to a stop.

"Why are we stopping," Dawn whispered, holding Josiah close to her heaving chest.

"Do you hear that?" Ferguson whispered. His dark hand cupped his big ear as he leaned on his black cane. His purple suit looked immaculate, even after all that running.

"Screaming," Carlos whispered. "What is that?"

"That's Little Heaven," Marlon whispered as he bowed his head.

"Now what?" Ferguson questioned loudly, throwing his lanky arms into the air.

"Keep your voice down," Ogre mumbled, standing next to his tall, thin angel. Her blonde hair looked as though she had just run a brush through it; not one twig or leaf littered her golden waves. She didn't seem at all winded, and her emerald dress blew weightlessly in the breeze.

There was a rustling coming from behind them. Their eyes widened with fear. "Everyone, cover! It's a speedster." No one moved as they all looked at each other. Ferguson smiled and shrugged his shoulders.

"What cover?" Ogre looked around passively. The alpine trees offered no protection for the giant, Ogre, the emerald princess, or the pimp in the purple suit.

Ogre pushed his woman behind him and pulled his bowie knives from his belt. Behind him Sheila hiked up her satin dress and untied the rope dart she had tied around her right leg. Ferguson pulled his sword from its cane hilt, and Marlon unhooked his morning star from his back. He held the club in his left hand in front of Dawn's face. She noticed the spikes were encrusted with a black substance. She tried not to think of that and held her daggers, ready for attack. Carlos had one hand on the tree and stared out into the forest, awaiting fate. His blue training shorts hung low on his knees; his grey muscle top was damp with sweat. He scratched at his Puerto Rico tattoo on his other arm before once again holding on to the tree.

A red blur came dangerously close before stopping suddenly in front of the group. The stop was so sudden it kicked red leaves five feet into the air, creating a fatal swooshing sound.

"Kelly," Marlon said, relieved.

The leaves died down, revealing a red-headed woman whose hair had all but come out of its neat braid. Her once-pristine white tank top and capris were smeared with blue, a deep, dark blue. Silver tears streamed down her face. "I have been looking everywhere for you," she cried.

"It's okay. You found us," Marlon assured her, hanging his weapon on his back.

Kelly glanced at Dawn and quickly looked away. "Your plan failed." She looked wearily into Marlon's face. "Everyone's gone. Jorge and Maribelle are in the caves hidden, a few clicks from here. Little Heaven is under attack. They took Lily." She began sobbing and then collapsed. Ogre caught her before her limp body hit the ground. Marlon stepped forward and took her body from Ogre into his own cradling arms.

"I got her," Marlon said solemnly. "I got her. Can you lead?"

Ogre nodded and they headed east. They saw the entrance to the cave as the sun began to set. It was partially hidden on the edge of a hill, covered in bushes and large boulders. A candle's soft light could be seen from the inside.

"I'll go check it out," Carlos said as he entered the cave, not having to bow as he skipped in. He hurriedly came back out. "Okay. Come on, hurry."

Once inside the cave, Dawn was surprised to see cots and tables set up. In the middle of the cave on a wooden table was one candle. She was not surprised to see that its flame illuminated the entire cave. Maribelle was lying on a cot against the right wall of the cave. Jorge was applying a pale-green putty to a wound on her leg.

"What happened?" Marlon asked, rushing over toward them after gently placing Kelly on a cot.

"We got attacked," Jorge said. "A hell bat took Lily. We were ambushed by Ghouls."

"What form did they take?" Ferguson asked.

"One was Mark. The rest, I'm not sure."

"I'm sorry." Marlon reached out his hand out to Jorge. Jorge took his hand and hugged Marlon. After releasing him he buried his pale face into his bony white hands.

"They are attacking us with our own family," he weeped.

"That wasn't Mark. You know that. It just looked like him." Marlon comforted him as he rubbed his back. Jorge gained his composure and wiped his eyes. "Ghouls shouldn't even be here. They are mid-level demons. And the hell bats too."

"I know," Marlon whispered as he looked down to the sleeping Maribelle.

"Where's the other group?" Jorge asked, suddenly aware. "Where's Elizabeth?"

Carlos cringed at the name. His skinny mustache went up in pain as he squeezed his eyes closed, trying not to remember. "Hell bat."

The group was silent for a long time. Most of them stared into space, either alone or curled up in one another's arms. Dawn sat on the floor at the back of the cave alone. Maribelle had woken up and asked to hold Josiah. Jorge said it was because she wanted to remember what she was fighting for, but in truth, she just loved him and had worried for his safety while the groups were separated.

Dawn tried hard to fight back the bad thoughts. She wondered silently where the others were. She didn't feel comfortable in a room that didn't have Ulrica sifting or Bancroft attempting smoke rings. Where was Kale, and did he have anything to do with the murders? Was Elizabeth still alive or did the hell bat eat her? What the hell was a hell bat anyway? Dawn felt clammy and sick with worry, and she knew the others did too.

"Twwweeeeee-twweeee." A whistling sound broke the silence. It was coming from outside of the cave.

Marlon and Jorge both stood, brandishing their weapons. Carlos whistled back, getting to his feet and putting his hand over the flame of the candle.

"We need some help!" Bancroft's gruff voice was heard before he was seen helping Samuel carry in Benjamin. Ulrica was behind them blowing powder and sprinkling dusts.

"Get him on a cot!" Marlon bellowed.

Samuel and Bancroft lifted Benjamin's lifeless body onto a vacant cot that stood against a wall.

"I've bandaged it pretty well, but the wound is very large and we had to keep moving," Ulrica said, working swiftly and emptying her bag on the floor in front of the cot.

Samuel took a seat at the wooden table and stared into the flame.

"There were demons," Ulrica said, "high-level demons." The remaining thirteen souls sulked, each looked at the other in weary defeat.

"Has anyone seen any high levels from our side?" Carlos asked. He was holding Kelly's hand as she lay still.

"No," Ulrica said as she bowed her head, pretending to look for the paste that was already in her hands.

"I know this isn't the time," Ferguson moved up to Ulrica who was busy sewing Benjamin's shell together as Bancroft caught the soul spilling out into a glass vial, "but what happened?"

"We were ambushed," Samuel said, still staring into the fire. "Andrew was the first. A reaper came, slashed him right in half." He put his black hand on his head. "We didn't even have a chance to save him. Then he went for Charlett, but my brother jumped in front of the sickle. Got slashed for nothing 'cause a hell bat came and took her anyway. I told her I had her back. Now she's gone." The massive man laid his head down and began to cry. Dawn walked over to him and placed her hand on his shoulders. He wrapped his mammoth arms around her slender waist and cried into her abdomen. She wrapped her arms around his head and let him wet her shirt.

"LILY!" Kelly woke up screaming. Blue beads of sweat were trickling down her forehead. "No, nooooo."

Carlos laid her back down and smoothed her hair.

"Shhhhhhh. Kelly, shhhhh," he whispered.

"Three gone, two kidnapped," Marlon whispered. "So where's Cowboy Bill."

"He said he had to get to Little Heaven," Jorge said. "He couldn't be persuaded otherwise."

"And Emitt?"

"Didn't feel right letting Cowboy Bill go alone," Jorge added.

"What do we do now?" Dawn whispered as she held Samuel.

"We rest," Ulrica said, her hands blue with soul.

"We leave in the morning," Marlon added.

"We have to make it to the mountain." Maribelle was sitting up, holding Josiah in her plump arms. "If we don't, this world will be gone. I saw it."

Chapter 15

Change of Plans

*D*awn was the first to wake, lying with her back flat against the cot. Josiah was on her chest fast asleep, rising and falling with every breath she took. The sun began to soar to its rightful place. The early-morning light began to flood the cave entrance. Its dull-orange luster illuminated the surroundings, and the cave walls began to sparkle. When Dawn looked closer, she saw the walls were littered with beautiful gems. Precious stones were sticking out from the ceiling and walls, which made the cave sparkle in the radiance of the sun. Dawn wanted to savor this peaceful moment. If her dreams were any indication of what was to come, today would be another day full of screams, pain, and tears. She took in the crisp, early-morning air and stared at the gemmed cave walls in silence, losing herself in their beauty.

"Just another day in paradise," Dawn whispered to herself as she held Josiah and stroked his bare feet. She knew there was much ground to cover today. She dared to glance over to the map Ferguson had drawn with his cane in the dirt last night. The fountain where the angels awaited them was half way up a mountain. The mountain itself was far away from the cave they took refuge in. The journey was to be long and treacherous, even without the monsters trying to kill them. She knew they had to make it there while the light of day still shone; according to Jorge there was not another secret hideout. The plan was never to need a secret hideout.

The night had been long and loud, an unfriendly environment for anyone trying to get rest. Nearly everyone awoke screaming at one point or another, from nightmares or pain. There were fears whispered in the dark of the demons that wanted their souls and the ones that just wanted to spill them. Dawn eventually gave up on sleep. One dream after another was filled with creatures that reached out to her from the dark; their red eyes glared at her from a corner. Monsters ripped her apart, piece by piece, and all the while Josiah screamed. Dawn had lain wide awake for most of the night. Her never-ending slew of questions was much more comforting than the crevices of her dark subconscious. Now that the morning rays were beginning to invade the cave, Dawn was in no hurry to move. She would much rather spend the rest of eternity staring into the gleaming gem walls than step foot outside the cave.

As the orange light grew into a bright white light, the cave became alive with the sounds of the others. Groaning and shuffling and more groaning. Whispers began to bounce off the walls, and Dawn could hear Bancroft tapping his pipe, getting ready for his morning smoke.

"Can I hold him?" Maribelle stood over her, her short curls bouncing below her ears. Dawn immediately noticed the pain and worry on Maribelle's normally happy and optimistic face. With only a glance, Dawn saw the sadness that filled Maribelle's deep-brown eyes.

"Of course." Dawn sat up and peeled Josiah off of her chest. His round face squinted at the morning light. His chubby face was marred with sleep marks from laying on her shirt, which made him look like an angry old man. "Good morning, little man." Dawn giggled as she handed Josiah over to Maribelle's open arms. Once in her embrace, Maribelle danced over to her cot, twirling as she held Josiah above her head. His laugh echoed throughout the cave. Everyone smiled at the sound, and for a moment, the atmosphere seemed brighter.

Upon seeing that Dawn was awake, Ulrica left a discussion with Bancroft and Marlon and came to take a seat next to her on the cot. Her hair hung carefree over her shoulder in a loose ponytail. Her character did not suggest that she was about to go to war. Had Dawn not known better, she never would have guessed it.

"We will be leaving soon. How do you feel?" Ulrica asked with a genuine smile.

Dawn sat with her head tilted toward the shimmering ceiling, her hands folded in her lap. "Scared."

"It's okay to be scared. As long as you are scared for the right reasons." Ulrica, too, became captivated in the glimmer of gems above them. "What do you fear?"

"Demons."

"Well, that's just silly," Ulrica said matter-of-factly.

Dawn broke her gaze at the ceiling and looked over at Ulrica, who stared back earnestly. She had meant what she said.

"Silly?! They are taking people and slashing people and changing into our *people* after they murdered them and . . ." Dawn's voice began to rise in both volume and pitch.

"Oh, don't get me wrong. I fear their actions too. I do not, however, fear them. That is what they want. The more you fear them, the stronger they are." Dawn gazed out of the cave's mouth; she let the sun blind her. She wanted so much for the cave to swallow her and keep her forever in its bejeweled stomach.

"Why do you think they chose to be so hideous?" Ferguson said from his cot. He rolled onto his belly, oddly resembling a schoolgirl with his feet crossed in the air, swaying behind his back. His hat was off and he was picking his small afro with a golden pick. "We are taught from the very beginning that ugly things are bad and evil and to be feared, and beautiful things are good and should be trusted." He paused as he rolled onto his back, dusting off his purple suit and putting his hands behind his head as a pillow. "I learned, after my third wife, that this is *not* true!" He chuckled to himself and whispered, "So beautiful and such a bitch!" He gazed at the ceiling, joining Ulrica, Dawn, and Maribelle in appreciating the rich beauty of their surroundings.

"Bottom line, you don't fight as well when you're scared," Ulrica said.

"But they have no reason to fear me," Dawn said and looked with frustration at her delicate hands.

"Being a monster is not the only way to intimidate someone," Samuel said from the table. "Do as the angels do, darlin'. Show no fear, no flaw. Let them believe that you are above them and therefore stronger than them." His muscular arms supported his head as he looked up into the sparkling ceiling. "If you can be stone cold as a crazy beast is hurdlin' your way, what do you think that says to the monster?"

"Why on earth isn't she scared?" Ferguson answered. "She must be stronger than me."

"A proud, courageous man will always fare better than a scared man in battle. No matter the size or situation." Bancroft invited himself into the conversation. "Sure, a scared man might make a few courageous moves once or twice, but a courageous man does so throughout the entire battle."

"Why are you all telling me this?" Dawn peered at the different faces, each turned up admiring the precious stones.

"Because you ain't seen nothing yet." Kelly arose from her cot. "How long have I been out, and where are the others?"

After Kelly and Benjamin were briefed on the situation, Ulrica checked Benjamin's wounds, which had, thankfully, almost completely healed. Ferguson and Marlon wielded their weapons. Maribelle helped Dawn into the sling. Jorge, who had been silent the entire time, was now whispering in a corner with Ulrica. They were holding hands and swaying from right to left. Kelly, dressed all in white, kneeled and dug a hole in the ground with her hands. She took a rock out of her pocket and buried it. She knelt on one knee and mumbled some words. One last tear rolled down her face and she rose. Dawn watched as she walked over to Carlos, who embraced her fully. He whispered something into her ear and kissed her lightly on the cheek.

"Listen," Marlon said, demanding attention, which he immediately received. "If we can go, with no stops, we can make it to the mountain by sundown." Marlon held his arms behind his back as he addressed his people. He resembled a combat commander, even though his black track pants and shirt were in no way uniform. "I *believe* we can make it." His jaw quivered as he tried to find the words to say. "We *have* to make it. Let us pray."

Dawn watched as they all closed their eyes and began to pray. Marlon raised his head to the sky and opened his palms. His lips moved and his brow creased. Carlos and Kelly took to one knee and bowed their heads, crossing their bodies with their right hands. Samuel, Ferguson, and Benjamin held hands in a circle. Maribelle sat with Joey, her lips mouthing the Lord's Prayer. All were praying except Ulrica and Jorge. They simply stood next to each other watching the others, like Dawn. She was instantly overcome with a wave of awkwardness. *Why am I not praying?*

After the prayer , there was much commotion as everyone hustled to get their weapons and belongings. When they were ready, they gathered in the front of the cave, nervously whispering to one another. Ulrica checked Maribelle's work and strapped Josiah tighter to Dawn's chest. As she tied a knot in the blanket, she whispered, "Why were you not praying?"

"I, I remembered all the days and nights I spent praying in my last life," Dawn whispered in return, "and look where that got me."

Ulrica smiled as she finished checking the last knot. Maribelle walked up to them. Her steps seemed heavy and her round eyes frowned; the happy sparkle was missing.

"Can I see him one more time?" she asked, looking up at Dawn. Dawn nodded and uncovered Josiah's face. Maribelle smiled a faint sad smile and leaned close to him. She whispered something in his ear before gently kissing his forehead. A lone tear escaped her eye before she walked toward the opening of the cave and joined the others. Dawn and Ulrica exchanged a worried look, but before either one of them could speak, Marlon began the journey.

Chapter 16

The End

They marched westward through the massive forest, climbing up and down mammoth tree-covered hills. Every now and then they heard screaming in the distance or a great whooshing sound above. Dawn nearly fainted the first time she spotted a hell bat flying over them through the forest canopy. It had a huge wingspan and looked too heavy to perch on any of the giant trees. It looked like it was easily big enough to pick up Marlon and swallow him whole. The bat's wings were long and thick and leathery, and his claws were a shiny black. The whole bat was black—black like midnight, black like fear, and black like death. She tried to remember what the others had said about not fearing. *What a joke.*

The forest floor began to slope downward again, forcing them to march slower.

"Watch your footing," Marlon whispered, reminding Dawn of the tree root that sent Carlos flying three hills ago. The leaves underfoot rustled as they half slid down the hill. Once at the bottom, Marlon pointed east in the direction of the ravine and everyone followed his lead. Dawn was very thankful not to be climbing another hill. There was always a sense of anxiety once they reached the top and before they saw the other side.

Dawn soon found the anxiety levels in the groove to be higher than the hills. There were no trees growing in the crevice, and there was less protection; she felt open to the elements. Anyone could be watching from atop the hills, and they would never be the wiser.

The group was moving faster now through the rusty, damp

leaves that covered the rocky river bed. Their feet sent whispers through the forest, daring to give away their position. Dawn found it difficult to find her footing, and she slipped a few times, sending smooth grey rocks skipping noisily across the gorge. Each time she sent a rock flying, she had to dodge the nasty looks from Jorge and Sheila. Only Ferguson offered her comfort. He looked back and smiled, seeming wildly out of place with his cane, dark purple suit, and wide smile. He stopped walking and waited for Dawn to reach his side. Once there, he stuck out his elbow. She accepted his invitation and hooked her arm to his. Together they walked in silence. She giggled silently, as they must have looked ridiculous strolling along the dry creek bed, arm in arm, Ferguson's golden tooth shining in the sun. In this moment, Dawn realized that she admired Ferguson. As he swung his cane back and forth, he was always in good spirits and constantly raised those of the people around him. Dawn wondered if he had always been this carefree and kind.

Clack-clack-click-clack-clack. A grey rock skipped past the gay couple from behind. The two looked over their shoulders to see the embarrassed face of Sheila glowing red in contrast to her golden hair. Ferguson snickered and gave Dawn's hand a good squeeze, then, without warning, he jumped at least two feet off the ground and clicked his heels together. Everyone smiled and Ferguson beamed.

The smooth riverbed rocks began to get bigger. The group now looked like kindergartners playing hopscotch, carefully tiptoeing from stone to stone. Ferguson was the biggest kid of them all, jumping from stone to stone and striking a pose with each stop. He kept his charades up until the stones got too big to skip from. The steppingstones were slowly replaced by large, grey, jagged boulders. They were no longer hopping, skipping, or gay. Their journey had become physical. Their progress was slow and grueling. Not only did they have to scale huge boulders, but they also had to climb uphill.

Dawn had to be helped up the larger boulders, being extra careful not to bump against Josiah as she made her way up. Benjamin and Maribelle also had to be helped for different reasons. Ulrica was worried that Benjamin's stitched wound, although mostly healed, would burst open if Benjamin overstretched. Maribelle was often too short to simply pull herself up like the others. Jorge and Kelly took turns giving her a boost. As they reached the top of the mound, Dawn looked down on boulder and waterfall she had just scaled, and felt a warm satisfaction of having accomplished a great feat. The breeze blew past her, making her feel strong and free at the edge of the butte.

As the last of the group helped Maribelle up the last boulder and dusted themselves off, Dawn turned to Marlon, looking for direction. She was immediately awestruck at what lay before them. A vibrant green-grass field swayed in the wind, freckled with beautiful wildflowers.

"So many different colors," Dawn whispered.

Huge pieces of rock jutted out of the ground. There were large jagged ones and smooth round ones. The field resembled a disheveled chessboard. Behind it stood one mountain, alone and defiant. Dawn smiled when she saw how close it was. The mountain shot into the white fluffy clouds that hid its true size. One side of the mountain had a huge chunk of its side missing, as though God got hungry and bit in to it. Dawn chuckled to herself as she imagined the scene. *The rocks we just climbed was His cookie-crumb trail. So messy!* Dawn thought playfully to herself.

Instead of going through the grass, the group veered left and stayed in the cover of the forest. Dawn kept looking longingly to the rocky meadow, envious of the flowers that got to sway freely to and fro in the breeze, being sun kissed all day.

The sun had arrived at its peak and shone through the tops of the trees. Dawn was alarmed to notice that she could now see her own shadow on the needles on the ground. The colossal, lustrous trees that had offered so much cover before were replaced by gangly pine trees. Even though she was exposed, she felt good to be able to feel the sun and see the sky. She smiled as she took in the scent of Christmas and then looked down at Josiah. His eyes searched the sky above them, and he seemed captivated by the way the sun shone and shadows fell. *I love this child.*

As their shadows became longer, the group walked faster. The only sound was that of their feet, marching along the forest floor. The sounds of screaming and fighting from the west were no longer heard. However, the feeling of dread remained. The forest had grown thin; the trees were skinny and too far apart from each other. Dawn could feel the tension intensify around her, and she felt as if she were being watched. A few steps more and she knew they were being watched, stalked.

The others knew it too. Without slowing or stopping the march, Marlon took his morning star off of his back and Ferguson unsheathed his slender sword from his cane casing.

Dawn looked behind her. Sheila's rope dart dangled freely from her right hand. Everything about her seemed to flow—her golden hair, her green dress, her essence itself. Everyone had taken out their weapons, without any hesitation. Dawn wrapped her fingers around the handles of her daggers and pulled them to her sides.

"Marlon." Bancroft boldly broke the silence. "Marlon, just stop. It's no use."

"We are so close." Marlon spoke through gritted teeth. "So close . . ." He lowered his head and sulked, sending his morning star thudding into the soft forest floor by his feet. "It's just over that hill."

"Hey, hey, buddy, it's not over yet." Bancroft went to him and lifted the morning star off the ground, quickly dropping it again. "Wow, that's heavy!" He chuckled deeply. Marlon raised his head and smiled. His massive arms grabbed Bancroft. Marlon squeezed him around the shoulders, burying Bancroft's head into his sternum.

"I love you, little man." Marlon smiled and squinted his eyes.

"I love you too, you big baby," Bancroft answered back, wiping the back of his hand across his face. "Now wipe those damn tears off your nose. You look ridiculous."

"Well, my friends," Carlos said, taking some rocks out of his pocket. "We have been surrounded." The group began to encircle Dawn; their weapons faced outward.

"In the event of my death . . ." Jorge said, holding his spear out toward the surrounding forest.

"Don't talk that way," Maribelle interrupted sharply, holding her sai by her side.

"SHOW YOURSELVES!" Marlon bellowed into the empty forest. Six large, hooded, black creatures came up from behind the trees and seemingly up from the ground. A black smoke billowed up from under their large hoods. Their eyes were beady and shimmered like black diamonds from behind the smoke. They advanced on the group, the cloaks covering their feet. The only visible parts of their bodies were their black and charred hands, holding long-handled sickles.

"Reapers." Kelly had one sword in each hand and two knives attached to her belt. She stood ready to attack, and not a shred of fear passed over her. "These guys killed Edward."

"And Mark," Carlos said as he looked back to the redhead.

"Watch the scythes; they are razor sharp and super fast," Kelly warned.

A high-pitched barking sound came from over the hill. Black shadowed blurs came running toward them on all fours.

"Grubs!" Carlos yelled. The grubs all halted in the distance. They sat like obedient monkey-dogs, waiting patiently for their masters to call on them.

"Kiiiiiiiiiiiiiiiiiiiii!"

"That's not all," Samuel said, pointing a finger toward the sky.

"Hell bats." Benjamin finished his brother's sentence.

"Well, ladies and gentlemen, it's been an honor," Ferguson said as he tipped his hat and raised his sword, taking a bow before getting into position.

Dawn stood in the middle with her daggers by her side, motionless, frozen with fear. There was a deep grumbling coming from behind her. Terrified, she dared herself to take a look.

"Grrrrrrrrr." Ulrica growled and then snapped. Her transformation was complete, and she stood ready, swaying from side to side.

The reapers attacked all sides at the same time. Samuel and Benjamin raised their oak staffs, metal point up, and clinked them.

"Cheers," they said simultaneously. The first blow was struck as they both smacked the first reaper in the head, sending his cloaked body sliding on the forest floor, leaving a black dirt trail eight feet long. The twins broke circle to pursue their enemy.

"Gaaaaaaaaaaaa!" The other reapers screamed as their comrade fell. All around her, Dawn could hear the clinking and clanking of metal against metal. In between it all, a red blur sliced the reapers through the middle. One by one they fell.

"It's like they not even trying," Ferguson yelled as he danced away in a sword fight. "I don't get it."

Dawn watched the grubs, and an eerie feeling came upon her. They each sat like stone monkey-gargoyles, watching the fight from a distance.

"It's a diversion!" Marlon yelled. "We have to make it up the hill!" Jorge yelled as he and Maribelle speared the second reaper through the chest. Blue metallic soul sprayed into the air and hung in front of Dawn.

"Their souls," Dawn whispered. "They look just like mine." The slain reaper fell on his back by Dawn's feet, and as the smoke began to drift out from under the hood, Dawn gasped and covered her mouth. "He . . ." she sputtered as she looked down at the face of a young man. He looked normal and peaceful in death. "He's just a man. He's just like us!" Dawn froze.

The twins grabbed her and escorted her up the hill. The rest followed suit, climbing the hill as they simultaneously fought the remaining four reapers.

Ulrica, still at the foot of the hill, jumped wildly onto the back of one of the reapers and clawed under its hood like a feral beast. Dawn watched as the reaper fell backward onto her. She scrambled in a manic fury onto its chest, pinning its shoulders down with her claws. In an instant, she dove her head into its hood. The screaming that came from the reaper as Ulrica violently ravished its head was sickening; its screams were ear piercing.

"If they didn't know we were here . . ." Samuel said, holding Dawn's arm tight as she doubled over onto her knees, dry heaving.

". . .they do now," Benjamin finished.

When Ulrica finally brought her head up, she was dripping with dark-blue soul. The heavier soul dripped down and onto her chest, and the lighter soul floated in the air around her head. Her hair was wet and her face unrecognizable.   At the sight of the metallic-blue soul, the cherry-brown grub closest to Dawn awoke and on all fours ran to the slayed reaper. Its eyes were an electric blue as it opened its mouth over the lifeless body Ulrica had left behind and greedily sucked in the soul that seeped out. Again, Dawn buckled over Josiah's bundle.

"They are just like us," Dawn whispered to Samuel, who still held her arm.

"Given the chance, they would do the same to you and Joey. We are damn lucky to have a vicious beast like Ulrica on our team," Samuel said with his head high, not even looking at Dawn. "Now get up and be strong."

Dawn slowly rose, trying to understand war, but mostly trying to erase the young man's face from her memory. She looked down at the bundle in her arms and realized Samuel was right. She watched as the others fought, gaining strength with every blow.

Marlon and Bancroft each fought their own reapers. Bancroft dodged blows, sidestepped swings, and looked for the right time to apply his ax. Marlon locked weapons with his opponent. Marlon freed a hand, pulled out his bowie knife, and sliced the arm of his attacker. There was another sickening screech as the creatures backed up. This was just enough diversion for Marlon to unlock his weapon and swing the spiked ball directly into the hood. The screeching stopped. As soon as the body hit the ground, a grub came and hovered over it. Its grey body shuddered as it hungrily sucked in the soul.

Bancroft too found the perfect moment and swung his ax deep into the hooded creature's rib cage. The creature fell at once to the forest floor, with Bancroft's broad ax still lodged in his side. Bancroft slammed his foot down on the creature's chest and yanked out his ax. With his foot still on the creature, he glanced over at Ferguson, who danced away with his partner.

"Ferguson, hurry it up, huh?" he grunted to his friend. With a swift flip of the wrist, Ferguson pierced the heart of his attacker and joined the group as it moved toward the top of the slope. The further away from the dead bodies they went, the closer the grubs moved. Their little hairy ape hands quickly found the source of the injury, and their mouths opened wide, exposing flat black teeth. Once they emptied the shells, they took off in the opposite direction, running in jagged, blurred lines, cheeks full like squirrels preparing for winter.

"That was too easy," Marlon told the others as they approached the top of the hill. "Something's not right." Marlon carried his club with a straight arm, keeping the still somewhat shell-shocked Dawn and the twins behind him as he tramped up hill, crossing one massive leg in front of the other.

"*Caaaaaaaaaaaaaaaaaaaaa!*" Another hell bat joined the two that circled above them like vultures over road kill.

Carlos was the first to make it to the top of the hill. The others watched as he swung, surprised by something hidden by the edge of the incline. He missed and fell to one knee.

"NOOOOOOOO!" he screamed before being cut in half by a wide-bladed sword that curved like a crescent moon.

Dawn froze and watched as the front half of Carlos came sliding down the hill.

"CARLOS!" Kelly screamed with grief as she sped up the hill, falling to her knees to meet his upper half.

"Run," Carlos breathed to her as his soul gushed onto the forest floor. A grey grub eagerly ran up the hill on all fours, hissing as he bared his black teeth.

"Get back!" Kelly screamed, swinging her sword. "You can't have him."

"*WEEEEEEEEEEEEEEEEEE*," screamed the monkey creature that pulled out his hair to get to the body. The creature screamed in torment as he watched the blue soul float upward like shimmering strings on an invisible balloon. He tested death, trying get closer to the wasting soul. His eyes glowed bright, as if pure lighting were trapped inside them. It hurt to look into his primate face. Another grub came from the other side.

"*WEEEEEEEEEEEEEEEEE.*"

"I'm sorry," Kelly whispered into the dead man's ear. She stood and looked at the group. Her green eyes looked silver through the tears. She sheathed her swords and took off in the opposite direction, a red blur riding the side of the hill like a wave.

"*CAAAAAAAAAAAAAAAAAW*," the hell bats called out. Grabbing Dawn's attention, the rest of the group stood motionless, watching the grub fill his mouth with Carlos.

"Don't you let them do that to me," Bancroft spat. "You just let the earth take me."

"Wha . . ." Dawn began, speaking out loud and pointing with a shaking finger to the top of the mound. "What's up there?"

"Step back," Jorge called out from the back of the group. Maribelle grabbed him by the arm.

"You are NOT going up there! We need you! You have to save

it!" she screamed as she pulled his arm back down to her.

Ferguson, Marlon, and Bancroft looked at him, and Samuel and Benjamin shook their head. Dawn stood clueless in the middle, watching as one grub fought another for the bottom half of Carlos. The hair on the napes of their necks stood on end as they shook in anticipation of feeding. The first one had blue seeping out his mouth; the other began to suck up the leftovers.

"You got any other ideas?" Jorge looked at the men. "Everyone has a purpose. Marlon, you taught me that."

"No, no, no." Maribelle was crying, shaking her head.

"*CAAAAAAAAAAAAW, CAAAAAAAAAAAAAAAAAAW!*" The twins looked up; the hell bats were growing impatient.

"If we don't get up to the top of that hill soon, we won't have any chance at all," Benjamin reasoned.

"We don't know what's up there," Ferguson added. "Make a hole."

"No," Maribelle threw an angry finger in Jorge's face. "No, we need you!" she pleaded as silver-blue tears streamed down her face. "I," she put her small hand over her big bosom, "I need you." Jorge threw his spear into the ground and took Maribelle's head into his hands.

"I will find my way back to you, I promise." He closed his eyes and kissed her. "I love you."

When he opened his eyes again, they were on fire, a bright orange that began streaming down his pale face like molten lead. He turned from the group, touching Ulrica's heaving shoulder on his way up the hill, singeing her hairs.

"Umm-hummm, na-ummm-hummm," he began chanting as he seemingly floated to the top of the hill. The leaves and grass turned to ash under his feet. "Be ready to run up! Get your weapons up!" Marlon commanded over Jorge's chant, which got louder with each step he took. "We have to take this hill!"

As Jorge made his way closer and closer to the edge of the

hill, the chanting became louder, and although Dawn could see no drums, she heard pounding in unison, a deafening drumming, as though there were an entire army drumming and chanting with them. Ulrica joined in chant and swayed to and fro as she growled. Maribelle chanted as well in a high-pitched voice in between sobs. Dawn wished she could escape the hillside, she wished she could be back in the tree, safe in Kale's arms.

"We will get him back," Ferguson whispered as he put his hand on Maribelle's shoulder and added his voice to thunderous tribal melody. Maribelle stopped crying and lifted her head; her eyes were toxic. She holstered her sai as she walked to her husband's spear. She picked it up, and with a loud crack, broke it in half along her thigh. With the spear in hand, she left the group and began walking up the hill on the parched leaves. Her pink slippers turning black with ash as she followed her husband's trail

"Make it worth what we have lost!" Maribelle didn't look back and began chanting, her voice was loud and strong. Then everyone joined in as they began walking up the side of the hill.

The drumming got louder and louder, feeding the suspense. The air around Dawn grew hot and thick. A blue fire began to grow around Jorge's feet. It swirled around him like a whirlwind, gaining speed with each step he took. He was almost at the top now. As he raised his arms straight out at his sides, the blue fire consumed him. He resembled a fiery cross at the crest of the hill. The heat he emitted burned everything around him, and it grew hotter and hotter. Dawn felt the heat on her shell. She could see the heat in the air, swirling, pushing the ashes higher and higher. The chanting was so loud now that all of their bodies seemed to sway with it.

Jorge reached the top of the hill and dropped his hands to his side with a loud clap. Dawn was pushed onto all fours. The twins and Marlon covered her body.

CRACK! A white-hot light shot from Jorge's shell, and for a moment, everything went quiet. The chanting was gone; the drumming was gone. And then, as if someone had decided to turn up the volume, screaming filled the air.

The screaming came from the top of the hill—excruciating, high-pitched wails and torturous screams of pain.

"NOOOW!" screamed Marlon, and the group stood and raced to the summit.

Everything within a fifteen-foot radius of the peak was blown away. Thick black smoke billowed from smoldering tree stumps and unrecognizable bodies. The hell bats screeched as they flew in and out of the pillars of smoke.

Dawn's eyes opened wide as she looked onto the destruction that Jorge left behind. Just beyond the devastation was what seemed to be a small army, and just beyond it was the mountain. She was relieved to discover that she was already halfway up the mountainside. She now stood in the crater she had seen mere hours before.

"You see that pool at the base of that cliff?" Ferguson yelled, smiling. "You only have to get there and the angels do the rest! That's it!" he said, slicing a reaper through the chest and sending soul flying weightless into the air. His movements were so perfect and exact; he was an artist in a purple suit, gracefully dancing through the enemies.

Dawn felt defeated. She did not share Ferguson's enthusiasm. She had reached the goal at last, but so had everyone else. Ferguson failed to draw this angry mob on his map at the cave. Now they shared this crater with many souls, and most of them were against her. As she looked about her, she saw giants that were taller than Marlon carrying meat cleavers the size of her body. Reapers with scythes and their hairy grey grubs, hungry for a feast. Dawn spotted a few of her old neighbors from Middle Haven. Ghouls, no doubt. Their eyes were blood red and unblinking. There were so many beasts, and all of them were furious that a bomb just blew away part of their army. An immense fear began to overwhelm her as she noticed that her enemies had begun to encircle them.

"DAWN! Get behind me and put up your daggers! We stay in a circle and we keep pushing until we reach that mountainside!" Marlon commanded as he attacked a ghoul that resembled a former neighbor. Bancroft and Ulrica went forward, taking lead of the group. Bancroft was agile and courageous as he swung his long ax into a giant that was three times his size. Ulrica hopped onto the back of another giant and savagely dug her nails into his neck. The giant grabbed her by the wrist and threw her onto the ground in front of him. Like a cat, she landed on all fours and sprung onto his chest, digging her sharp teeth into his face.

"Keep moving," Sheila yelled as she threw her dart out and reeled it back in, piercing the eyes and hearts of her enemies with uncanny accuracy. Ogre blindly swung his club and fist into the oncoming crowd. Shimmering soul flew through the air in every direction, until it seemed like they were wading through it. The grubs were gluttonous as they collected their prizes they had no part in earning.

They fought their way through. Samuel and Benjamin took over at the front of the group, parting the horde like the Red Sea. The group pushed its way closer and closer to the base of the cliff.

"Caaaaaaaaaaaw!" Dawn looked up to see a hell bat swoop down with its black leather wings spread; it had zeroed in on its prey.

"SHEILA!" Dawn screamed. Shelia looked up, eyes wide, and tried to dodge the incoming claws. The hell bat missed her body but still got her arm.

Sheila screamed in pain as she was ripped off the ground. The beast carried her swiftly up and over toward the forest. Dangling by one hand, she took the dart in her other and buried it deep into the underbelly of the beast. It began to spiral out of the air and crashed into the forest below.

"AAAAAAAAAAAAAAAAAAAARG!" Ogre roared as he went berserk, fighting his way to the forest, killing all who stood in his way. He sprinted into the trees in the direction of the screaming bat.

"Close that hole!" Bancroft yelled to the remaining fighters. The group quickly shifted as it struggled to fill the space. Dawn counted the remaining members of her group. What used to be twelve was now seven.

"We are seriously outnumbered, brother," Benjamin called out as he punched his staff through an enemy.

"We are so close," Marlon cried as he brought the spiked ball of his morning star down on an enemy head.

All around her souls were fighting and dying. Dawn had one hand on Josiah, rocking him gently. He hadn't cried at all; he hadn't made one sound. It was then Dawn realized that once again, it wasn't she who comforted him, but he who comforted her. She stopped rocking him and looked down at the bundle. He had her braid in his fat hand and casually sucked it. *Not a care in the world.*

The group had become stagnant and was no longer moving forward. They were so close. When Dawn looked up, she could see the cliffs towering over them, and she swore she could smell the fresh spring water from the fountain.

"That fountain may as well be a thousand miles away," Benjamin said as they were being pushed tighter into a ball.

"I failed." Maribelle had tears of sorrow streaming down her face. "I failed him."

"We failed," Samuel said as he raised his staff, preparing to fight to the death.

A red blur came up from behind them, cutting through their opponents on the way. Kelly stopped in front of the twins. "Hey, guys." She twirled her swords. "Miss me?"

"Hey, babe," Ferguson smiled. "You picked a rotten time to come back."

"I know," she grinned, "but I brought friends!"

"Eeeeeee-weeeeeee!" Orange birds swooped down, blowing fire onto the enemy.

"Yeeeeeee-hawwwww!" Cowboy Bill jumped down from the

back of a phoenix and joined the fight.

"What the hell took you so long?" Bancroft shouted up to Griffen. The fighting commenced. Not one blow was wasted as the group exploded outward onto their opponents. Dawn followed Marlon, who bulldozed his way to the pond, taking full advantage of the diversion.

He stopped dead in his tracks, and Dawn bumped into his back. Had she not had a protective arm around the baby, Josiah could have been hurt. She could hear the trickling of a small waterfall. *Are we there already?* Dawn thought. Marlon took a step back and kept Dawn behind him with a protective arm as his other arm prepared to swing his weapon. *Something is wrong. We are so close. Why is he backing up?* Dawn thought. She peeked her head under Marlon's arm and to her dismay saw three giants standing between them and the water. Dawn realized in despair that for the first time since she had entered this realm, Josiah was in real danger.

The three giants all wore Viking helmets that fit loosely on their large heads. Their leather vests were open and revealed hairy stomachs. The smallest of them was as tall as Marlon, and they each wore a victorious grin. *They're going to win.* Tears began to spill down Dawn's face. She was so close she could almost taste the clean, sparkling water that pooled behind the giants. The giants formed a semicircle around the two. Dawn looked around to see where the rest of her warriors were. Everyone was lost in war. Fear washed over Dawn's body. She clutched Josiah closer to her and held up her dagger in defense, as he tears began to soak the bundle in her arm.

After seeing Dawn, the smaller giant, who stood in the middle, winked as he tipped his helmet and blew her a kiss. The other two found his antics entertaining and began to laugh and smile with their toothless grins. **WHACK!** Marlon swung his morning star without warning and hit the tallest of the three in the head. Dawn seemed to see everything in slow motion; she watched his Viking helmet fly off in a spray of silver-blue soul. Some of his soul sprayed left and splattered the still-laughing faces of the other two dimwitted giants. She watched as his body began to tip. It seemed as though she could see every single piece of his golden-blond hair blow in the wind as he crashed down with a loud thud. "BROTHER!" the smallest giant screamed, revealing his light-blond hair as he threw off his helmet. In grief he fell to his knees, trying to keep the soul from further flowing up and out of his brother's mashed face. Dawn had just enough time to notice that the fallen brother's face had been knocked clear off. Then Marlon pushed her hard, causing her to fall on her back.

"That was a mistake," whispered the giant who stood in front of Marlon. He watched, as if frozen in time, as his smaller brother tried frantically to scoop the soul off of the dirt and into a small leather pouch.

Dawn scampered backward on the ground, clutching Josiah in one arm and her dagger in the other. She watched as Marlon swung at the giant in front of him; she hoped he would catch him off guard as well. The giant turned his gaze just in time to see the ball of Marlon's weapon fly toward his face. He dodged the blow in the nick of time, giving new meaning to saving face. The morning star smashed into his horned helmet and sent it flying clear over the trees and into the bushes behind Dawn.

The force of Marlon's unsuccessful swing sent his massive body spinning. He was now facing a wide-eyed Dawn. She watched in horror as the enemy took his spiked staff and smashed it into Marlon's side.

"Nooooo!" Dawn screamed, holding the dagger up to her quivering mouth. She watched as Marlon fell to his knees like a heavy stone. His opponent stood behind him victorious, a towering mountain. Marlon's eyes glazed over and looked as though someone had pulled a silver screen. As he closed his eyes, he sent tears rolling down his brown face, washing the dirt down with them.

"I'm so sorry," he said to Dawn as he opened his eyes. Dawn watched as the soul from his side ran through his fingers and floated upward in little drops.

"ARRRRRRR!" screamed his opponent before kicking Marlon in the back of the head with his enormous, brown, soul-splattered boot. The brutal blow sent Marlon flying forward and landing in between Dawn's legs.

"NOOOOOOOOOOOOOOOOO!" Dawn screamed as she sat defeated, trying to pull his head into her lap with one hand.

"Run," Marlon sputtered, as he coughed up blue weightless liquid.

"No. I am not leaving you," she said, holding her hand over the gash in Marlon's head.

"You have to," he managed.

"It's not worth it," Dawn said, shaking her head. Her face was blue with the different souls that had been lost in this war. She looked up to see the giant watching her, smiling. The giant held his staff like a baseball bat and patted it on his heavy hand. To her left she saw only fighting as far as she could see. Wounded shells lay on the ground, lifeless. There were so many spilled souls that it looked as though the survivors were all fighting underwater in a murky-blue lake. "It's just not worth it," she said again as the vengeful giant helped his smaller brother up off the ground. She looked over to her right. The fountain flowed, peaceful and serene, as if it were just a mirage. She looked back to the giants who were coming closer and drawing their weapons, and finally, she looked down at Marlon. He had his massive blue hand over her tiny one, trying to keep his soul in his head. And although he wasn't crying out loud, his silver tears washed his face. "I will not leave you," Dawn promised and kissed him on his forehead.

The shadows of the brothers cloaked them as they closed in. Dawn took her hand off of Marlon's wound and picked up the dagger. Full of rage and anger, fear and sorrow, she threw it at the tallest giant. Not to her surprise, the dagger missed him by five feet and planted itself deeply between his brother's blue eyes.

"Good throw!" Marlon cheered, sounding almost like his normal self. Infuriated, the tallest brother advanced, clutching his staff, prepared to send Dawn's head sailing. Dawn looked straight into his cold eyes; she braced herself for the hit. She was determined not to let him see any fear in her eyes. That satisfaction he would not have. There would be no pleading, no crying.

Before he could reach her he stopped, smiling even more sinister than before.

"I am going to enjoy watching you die," he said wild eyed and dropped his staff to his side. "You and your friend."

From out of the woods and behind the bushes came five snarling Gidlies. They each went in separate directions, but one dreadlocked wolf with fur the color of dried blood and with searing red eyes came directly to Dawn. She reached out a trembling hand as he approached her, growling and snarling viciously. His saliva hung off his jutted bottom jaw and dripped on Marlon's face.

"Holy . . ." Marlon squirmed and held on tightly to Dawn's waist. Terrified and helpless, he watched as the Gidly sniffed the bundle strapped to Dawn's chest and then licked her face. As Marlon watched Dawn grab the hound by the scruff of the neck, his jaw dropped. He watched in disbelief as her delicate hands got lost in the thick, dark fur and as she brought his massive snout directly toward her face and kissed him in between his red eyes.

Confused, the vengeful giant's arrogant smile faded as he processed what he had just witnessed. He was too late in raising his staff. The Gidly swiftly pounced on him and ruthlessly tore out his throat, leaving him no time to scream.

Marlon held his head as he sat up and wiped the drool off of his face. "The Gidly are helping us?" he questioned, still holding his leaking head. "Did you just hug a Gidly?"

"I swear I'll explain later," Dawn reassured him as she helped him tie his black shirt around his head.

Bancroft and Ferguson came rushing in, grabbing Dawn under

her arms. "It's now or never. More are coming!" Bancroft yelled.

Marlon, Bancroft, and Ferguson hurriedly escorted Dawn to the crystal-clear spring.

"Get in!" Bancroft yelled as he ushered Dawn to the water with flailing arms.

Dawn walked into the water. It wasn't a mirage; it was real. The water was cool, and the bottom of the pond was littered with smooth turquoise stones. She stopped halfway in. The water felt like a miracle, and she just wanted to immerse herself fully. She turned to see her friends, smiling and holding one another as they cried tears of joy. She smiled back and turned to continue walking into the pond. As she walked, she unwrapped Josiah's face.

"We made it," she whispered as she stepped deeper into the water. Josiah laughed. His eyes sparkled as radiant as the stones on the bottom of the pond. Dawn was waist deep when a ray of golden sunlight broke through the clouds at the top of the mountain. In that very instant, Dawn could hear a wailing. There were unholy screams of anguish and despair as the light washed over Dawn and Josiah. The enemies were defeated. The whole mountain was aglow, and Dawn stood in the middle of the light, looking up into it. It was so bright, but there was no need to squint. In the light she watched as another white light began making its way down. The wings of an angel spanned above her, their majestic white feathers promised an end to all the suffering. He floated down the mountainside, armed with a golden bow and golden arrows. He shot at the demons below him with divine accuracy. Each arrow gifted a tortured scream from the enemy. They began to retreat with haste back north to the forest. They had lost.

The angel's feet sent golden ripples through the water as he joined Dawn. She looked into his face and smiled as he held out his hands. Dawn untied Josiah and held him gently in the water. She smiled as she scooped the water into her cupped hand and washed it over Josiah's head, letting it roll off his blonde curls before bringing his wet smiling body to hers. She filled her lungs with his scent before kissing him on the bridge of his button nose. The angel wore a flawless smile as Dawn placed Josiah into his arms. He looked into Dawn's eyes, and without moving his pink lips, asked her, "Do you want to join us?"

Dawn looked behind her. Marlon's kind face was nodding her on. Ferguson was waving goodbye as he held on to Bancroft, who beamed and blew her a kiss. She sweetly smiled at her friends and mouthed "I love you." She turned back to the angel and reached out her hand.

SNAP! A large metal arrow broke through Dawn's chest, and with a metallic clang, it opened into a claw. Blue soul sprayed over the angel's white garments and splattered onto his pristine wings and Josiah's naked body.

Josiah screamed so loud the mountain shook. Boulders began to tumble down the mountainside. Dawn's eyes grew wide and her limbs flew forward as she was harpooned into the air.

Marlon fell to the ground and looked to the sky to watch her lifeless body fly over him, dangling from a rope. A demon, riding on a hell bat, blew a golden horn three times and carried her away. Upon hearing the horn, the rest of the enemy army below him immediately stopped fighting and retreated into the woods.

Griffen went after her, a blot of orange in a blue, misty sky.

"CAAAAAAW!" He was cut off by three hell bats that viciously snapped at him, pushing him back each time he tried to advance. He stopped only after a hell bat gashed his wing. Griffen fell to the ground, landing hard, and cried up to the sky.

"KEEEEEEEEE!" he screeched, his head craned toward the heavens. As the feathers on his head began to turn blue, the color washed all the way down to his tail, leaving only his chest orange.

The angel silently rose up into the light, taking the screaming baby with him. Boulders fell as storm clouds began to circle the mountain. The light was gone; the sun was now covered with angry clouds. All at once it began to pour. The heavy rain pushed all the spilled souls out of the sky and down to the ground. An ocean of blue replaced the green grass.

The only sound to be heard was the falling of the rain and thundering of the boulders crashing off the mountain.

Chapter 17

The Defeated

Marlon sat on the soft ground under the ancient oak. He placed little rocks around an oak sapling. He smiled as he stroked its tiny, bright-green leaves. He looked up to see Kale come out of the forest to meet him.

"Dawn's in Hell," Kale said. "I swear to you, giant . . ."

"Marlon," Marlon whispered.

"Marlon, I swear to you, I will free her." Kale looked down at the sapling. "She did that, didn't she?" He smiled, losing himself in a memory. When he brought his dreadlocked head back up, he was no longer smiling. "Until then, you and yours should not cross paths with any Gidlies."

Marlon nodded as he lay next to the tree and watched as Kale disappeared into the woods.

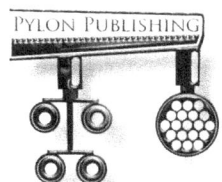

Are you an aspiring Author?

Getting published shouldn't be a dream

Pylon Publishing LLC specializes in the publication of experienced and aspiring authors alike. The small and knowledgeable company can provide the most custom and specialized services necessary to turn your manuscript into a book quickly and effectively. Since Pylon Publishing works directly with the word's largest wholesale book distributor, Ingram Book Company, authors can feel at ease with the widest distribution - Amazon, Barnes and Noble, etc.

It is Pylon Publishing's goal and mission to give authors the most flexibility, distribution, and earnings for their work. As a result, every author retains full control of their book upon publication.

That's the Pylon Promise!

www.ingramcontent.com/pod-product-compliance
Lightning Source LLC
Chambersburg PA
CBHW061231170626
46809CB00007B/2623